I0666484

"The Heart the Cowboy Broke"

McGuire Family Book Two

MJ Andrews

Table of Contents

FOR ALL THOSE MENDING A BROKEN HEART AND THOSE PRAYING FOR A SECOND CHANCE.

Praise for "Healing the Heart of a Cowboy"

"I loved the characters in this story! They were so fun to get to know. I loved laughing my way through their love story! It had just the right amount of thrills and discord. It was easy to follow and such a fun ride!" - River (Goodreads Reviewer)

"Thank you for such a wonderful story. This is a wonderful western romance, filled with some laughter and some mystery." - Genevieve (Goodreads Reviewer)

"I loved the characters in this story! They were so fun to get to know. I loved laughing my way through their love story! It had just the right amount of thrills and discord. It was easy to follow and such a fun ride!" - Melissa Newell Wootton (amazon.com)

"This is a really nice story of love conquering all...in spite of a shaky start! A heroine with a tough exterior but a soft heart and a hero who is every woman's dream make this an enjoyable escape into a credible and well described world." -

Clara (amazon UK)

Chapter 1

"I can't believe we're finished!" Lexi squealed, as she embraced her best friend, Valerie, in the hallway of Silverton High School. It was the last day of school and both of them were headed off to different colleges in the fall.

"I can! I'm so ready to make this world my bitch!" Valerie admitted confidently. Valerie was the typical popular girl that everyone had in high school. She sported long blond locks that she'd tarnished with pink streaks. Her delicate facial features were accentuated by her greenish-blue eyes that were the demise of any boy within a five-mile radius. Valerie wasn't a snob or bitchy and that was where the stereotype ended because she was sweet and would do anything for anyone.

Lexi leaned against the bright blue

lockers as Valerie cleaned out her own for the last time. Lexi and Valerie had been friends since middle school when Valerie punched CeCe Drake in the face for calling Lexi a four-eyed ugly duck. They'd been inseparable ever since. It was seen as an odd friendship given that Lexi was the complete opposite of her BFF in every way. With long dark brown hair that laid flat on her head, hazel eyes that were nothing to write home about and a body built like a teenage boy, she rarely turned heads. Add into the equation the braces and glasses and she might as well be invisible to the opposite sex.

"So Lex, what kind of trouble are we getting into tonight?" Valerie smirked as she waggled her perfectly shaped eyebrows.

Lexi rolled her eyes and pulled her gaze down the hallway where other students chatted together. The excitement and energy of the last day of school bounced off the walls that had been their home for the last several years.

"Honestly, I just planned to stay home tonight and get started on some advanced reading for the fall semester."

Valerie slammed the door to her locker and posed her hands on her hips as though she was Wonder Woman. Her eyes sharpened pinning Lexi in place.

Shit... She had that constipated look going on. A sure sign that she was about to argue with her.

"Sweetie, don't you think it's time for you to let me give you a makeover? Have one fling before you rush off to NYU in the fall? I mean, it's our last summer of freedom Lex! Let's do something wild!" she said, her eyes twinkled with excitement.

A large tanned arm made its way around her waist as Brett leaned in to plant a kiss on Valerie's lips. Brett Jenson was the star quarterback with beautiful black hair, blue eyes, and shoulders that needed a spread in GQ.

"I hear you want to do something wild. Did I hear that correctly?" Brett asked with the low husky voice that had all the girls swooning — all the girls, except Lexi. Brett was an awesome guy, sure, but he didn't do it for her and he spent far too much time looking at himself in the mirror. She was convinced he kissed his reflection good night.

"Babe, I was just trying to persuade Lex to let me help her with her hair and makeup so she can come to Colin's party tonight," Valerie declared wrapping her arms around Brett's neck. Brett turned his head toward Lexi as if only noticing that she was there for the first time.

"Lex, you should totally come along. You spend too much time with your nose in the books! Time to let loose and celebrate!" his gaze wandered to something over Lexi's shoulder. She turned to see what had captured his fleeting attention. Her heart stopped for a brief moment at the sight of the Adonis in living color swaggering towards them.

Sawyer McGuire.

It was as though the earth ceased to turn and all the oxygen was sucked out from her lungs. He caught her eye and offered a coy smile that instantly made her core throb with need and butterflies sprang to life in her stomach.

"McGuire!" Brett hollered breaking the spell she was under.

Sawyer stopped and stood next to her as he chatted with Brett about some football stats. But she didn't pay attention. She reminded herself that her lungs needed air and inhaled deeply. God, he smelt so good. It was a combo of Adidas for men, fabric softener and hay. His light brown hair was longer and moved freely, like a slow-motion video of Justin Bieber. And his eyes... he owned the most beautiful jade green eyes she had ever seen. In fairness, all the McGuire kids had green eyes that were show-stopping. But Sawyer's differed from his siblings because of the little flecks of gold around the outer circle.

A hand clasped around her shoulder and she was shaken out of her daydream. Only to realize that her gaze had been fixated on Sawyer.

"I'm sorry," she apologized before embarrassment forced her to look at her shoes, "did you say something?" Sawyer chuckled and a blush crawled slowly up her neck.

"I was just wondering if you'll be joining us for Colin's party tonight. I don't think I've ever seen you outside of school since middle school," Sawyer cleared his throat and shoved his hands in his pockets.

Lexi looked up and caught his gaze before glancing at Valerie who widened her eyes as if to communicate that she should say yes.

"Um, sure," Lexi nodded. He could've asked for one of her kidneys and she still would've agreed. Sawyer grinned and her heart stopped beating.

"Good! I'll see you guys there!" he said, punching Brett in the shoulder before walking away, leaving Lexi to oogle the deliciously firm rear he was sporting.

"Giiiirrrllll.... Now you've got to let me work my magic! That boy is fine," Valerie dragged out the word fine as though she belonged in the Bronx and not a cul de sac in Silverton's rich district.

Lexi sighed and her friend wrapped her arms around her shoulders and walked towards her car. Lexi didn't understand the big deal about makeup and hair products. If someone was going to be interested in her, then it shouldn't matter what she looked like... right?

That was exactly the argument she was having with Valerie an hour later as she sat cross-legged on Valerie's bed while she raided her huge walk-in closet for a party dress.

"I hear what you're saying, Lex. But you want to make an impression on a guy before you ever open your mouth to spew your quirky little brain," she argued from inside her closet.

"Ah-ha! This will be perfect!" Valerie rushed out, holding an emerald green sequenced party dress that cut low into a V in the front and sat about mid-thigh. It was completely outside her comfort zone, but she'd told Valerie that she would be open to anything.

After an hour and forty-five minutes, Valerie waxed her eyebrows, painted her face and managed to find a strappy gold-toned wedge that Lexi could walk in. She curled Lexi's hair in loose wavy curls, which was strange for her since she was a ponytail girl all the way. Valerie took another hour to get herself ready, curled her hair, applied makeup and zipped into a bright blue mini skirt, silver tube top and silver heels that Lexi would fall to her death in if she ever wore.

Valerie slipped a flask into her purse since her parents were out of the country on business, so she had free rein of the house and staff.

"You should probably call your mom and tell her you'll be sleeping over tonight," Valerie instructed, climbing into her bright green Jeep Wrangler.

"Good idea!" she said, pulling out her cell phone from her purse and calling her mother. They were accustomed to her staying over at Valerie's house, so they didn't even question it. Plus, she'd never done an irresponsible thing in her life and they didn't expect her to break any rules.

By the time they pulled up to the house party, the sun was setting. The party was already rowdy and there were people all over the front lawn, couples made out and guys drank beer. Lexi and Valerie made their way into the house, pushing and walking over people as they went. Colin Kincaid's parents were both from old southern money and they had a huge two storey house with all the bells and whistles. There was a gourmet kitchen that was used to hold a variety of alcohol. A pool lit up the back yard where numerous loungers were spread around and a fire pit to the side.

As soon as they made their way into the house, Valerie ran to Brett who was playing beer pong with Sawyer. She greeted her boyfriend, and by greeted she meant she tried to suck his face off. Feeling awkward, Lexi stood to the side hoping no one noticed her. Unfortunately for her, Colin noticed.

"Holy fuck...is that Lexi?" Colin's shocked expression and loud voice drew all the attention to his line of sight. Her.

Jesus fucking Christ.

Lexi gave a geeky wave to everyone as a vicious blush climbed her face. She wasn't used to people taking notice of her. Colin's eyes slowly ran over her body causing her to squirm. Despite being pretentious, she didn't have an opinion of Colin, but something about the way he looked at her like she was his next meal, had the hair on her neck standing up.

"Hey Lexi!" someone shouted, and she turned to see who bellowed, only to find Sawyer waving in her direction.

"Come play beer pong with me? I need a new partner now that Brett and Val are attached by their tongues," she laughed and nodded.

She hastily made her way to the beer pong table where Sawyer greeted her with a smile.

"You ever played before?" he asked.

"I haven't," she admitted.

He smirked, "It's okay I can teach you."

For the next hour, she and Sawyer played as a team and were in the lead when it was down to the last team of partners. She'd lost track of how many beers she'd consumed but she knew she'd done more laughing and smiling with Sawyer than she had in a long time.

The game was tied with each team

having only one cup standing. It was Lexi's turn and Sawyer pulled her into a huddle, forcing their heads closer together. The smell of alcohol permeated the air around them and the crowd grew silent.

"You got this Lex. You've been on fire all night!"

"It's strange because I'm not good at sports," she laughed.

"Well, you're a pro at beer pong. Let's win this!" he encouraged. She nodded and picked up the little white ball. She cracked her neck as if preparing for a fight and Sawyer moved behind her and rubbed her shoulder while he whispered in her ear. His touch was orgasmic, not that she'd had one of those, but she would have given anything to keep his hand on her skin.

"You got this Lex!"

He stepped back and the other team tossed their ball. The guy who stood on the other side of the table was intoxicated and she was sure someone supported him so he could stand. His wonky toss didn't even come close to their cup. If she sank hers, they won the game.

The crowd grew silent as Lexi prepared to aim. She focused and on her exhale let go of the ball. It moved slowly through the air until the splashing sound of the ball hitting the beer rang out. Cheers filled the house and the next thing she knew Sawyer had lifted her into his arms and twirled her around in celebration.

Once the crowd went about their business, Sawyer released his grip on Lexi and she slowly slid down his hard body. Their gazes locked and she saw the desire in his eyes as he inched closer to her. He flicked his gaze between her mouth and her eyes as if asking permission. Her breath hitched as he moved closer. His hands rose to sit on her cheek as he caressed the side of her jaw.

"I'd like very much to kiss you, Lexi. Is that okay?" he asked, his voice was husky and rough. All she did was nod because her brain couldn't process what her mouth would say.

He closed the gap between them and brushed his hot full lips over hers. He was tentative at first and pulled back. But the current charged through her body and the liquid courage in her blood made her spontaneous and she was not ready for the kiss to end. She pulled him into her again and demanded his response. His arms wrapped tight around her waist and time seemed to stop as they devoured each other in sensual perfection. His tongue ran across her lips causing her to gasp in surprise. He wasted no time slipping in to caress her tongue with his.

She moaned into his mouth as her body melted into his. Then he pulled back, leaving her craving the warmth of his touch. Both panted in anticipation when Sawyer wrapped his fingers around hers and pulled her through the crush of the crowd to an empty upstairs bedroom. He shut the door and pulled her into his arms.

"I've been wanting to kiss you since middle school," he confessed, pressing kisses to her nape.

"Why haven't you?" she whispered.

"Because I didn't think you liked me," he conceded, as she shook her head in surprise.

"I've always liked you, Sawyer. Kiss me again," she begged. It was as though she had no control over her body. She convinced herself that it could be a dream and wasn't happening. But then she felt the heat of Sawyer's body and concluded it was very, very real.

"We won't do anything you don't want to do, Lexi. I won't take advantage of you," he murmured.

"Just touch me, Sawyer," she demanded, rising on her tiptoes and capturing his lips in a scorching kiss. He turned and pushed her against the door as the heat began to pool in her panties.

Sawyer McGuire wanted her.

The four-eyed ugly duck.

He growled as her hands found the waistband of his jeans and she slipped her hands under to touch his skin. And abs... For the love of God...he really was an Adonis. She quickly yanked his shirt over his head to get a better view of the body she fantasized about. Her hands ran over the hard planes of his pecs and the bumpy hardness of his six-pack. It should be illegal to look that damn good.

His lips caressed the spot behind her ear as his hands moved to slide down the straps of her dress exposing her breasts and hardened nipples to the air. He kissed farther down until he sucked a pink perky nipple into his warm eager mouth. Sucking and licking with such intensity she reached for his hair and drew him closer to her body, demanding more.

"Oh, God..." she moaned, as he moved up her body to take her lips again.

"What do you want, Lexi?" he asked his voice low and rough.

She'd thought a lot about how she wanted to lose her virginity and she couldn't think of a better person than Sawyer. He was always the one in her dreams and realistically, she knew her virginity was not a big deal. At least not to her, so why couldn't she give in?

"I want you, all of you, Sawyer," she breathed against his lips, and that was all the permission he needed to reach down and slide her panties to the floor. When he stood he undid his jeans and she grasped his hard cock in her hands, eliciting a groan of satisfaction from him.

He yanked her closer for another hot kiss while his hands traveled down her body. He pushed up her dress to gain better access while she continued to stroke him in swift motions. He glided his fingers into her slippery folds and gently skimmed her clit. She jolted in surprise by the sensation and bit down on his lower lip. He circled her swollen nub before inserting his finger into her core, keeping his thumb stimulating her clit.

"Oh, fuck... don't stop," she cried, as she increased the pressure of her hold on his dick. He moaned and nuzzled his face into her shoulder as they both pleasured each other. He slipped in another finger and thrust inside her over and over until she gripped his shoulders in desperation and rode out her climax.

He reached for the condom in his back pocket and covered himself before using his knee to open her thighs.

"You're sure?" he asked. She nodded permitting him to continue. Without saying another word he gently inserted himself into her heat. There was a sharp pinch of pain, but it quickly eased as he moved gracefully inside her. His thrusts increased and her hips rose to meet his.

"Fuck, Lexi... I'm going to come," he muttered.

"Please Sawyer..." she plead, as she felt her body start to shake with ecstasy. His thrusts increased and he grunted loudly. Her core clenched around him as her body trembled with release and then he came with a loud sexy moan.

He pressed a chaste kiss to her lips before they both dressed. He opened the door he asked her to wait to come out until the coast was clear. She agreed, thinking it was because he was trying to protect her reputation as the boring book nerd.

She made her way down the back stairwell and decided to get some fresh air. Rather than go through the crowd she walked outside around the house to the back gate. She was walking along when she heard Sawyer's voice, with Colin and Brett.

"Dude, where did you run off to?"

Colin asked.

"I saw you leaving with Lex, did you guys hook up?" Brett asked a sharp tone indicated his protectiveness.

"Fuck no. Sawyer wouldn't do that. That girl needs a bag over her head if she's going to get fucked," Colin sneered.

"Man, you couldn't pay me to touch that," Sawyer shook his head in disgust.

Lexi stepped out from the shadows and Brett noticed her, but Sawyer's back faced her. She heard his words clearly.

"Who would ever want to date her anyway? She's not exactly the hottest girl around and she's always been a geek. No, she's definitely not what I want to screw around with," Sawyer said.

Despite the hurt that clutched her heart, Lexi continued to listen. Brett tried to relay to Sawyer to shut up, but he didn't catch on until Lexi tapped him on the shoulder. He spun around and his eyes grew wide.

"You really feel that way, don't you?" Lexi asked, her anger flared in her chest. Lexi tried hard not to cry in front of the dickheads.

"Lex," he started, moving towards her and Lexi took a firm step back. She held up her hand to stop him.

"You know what Sawyer, I always found you to be kind to everyone. But now I realize that all of it was an act. You're no better than Colin, with his pretentious and conceited personality. And let's be honest, you'd stick your pencil dick in anything for a cheap fuck," she growled, as her eyes filled with tears and a sob tunnelled up her throat.

Sawyer reached out to grab her wrist as she attempted to walk away, but she ripped her hand from his grip.

"Do. Not. Touch. Me," she snapped. "I don't want to see or speak to you ever again. Brett, let Val know I left, okay?" she asked. He nodded because he knew her well enough to know that it was best people stopped talking.

Heartbroken and humiliated, she turned and without a second thought ran. She was distraught as she ran, tears flowed freely down her face as she gasped to catch her breath. The bastard played her and it hurt like hell. She was running back to her house when she came to the crosswalk. She had the walk sign so she quickly stepped off the curb.

The sounds of broken glass, screeching metal and the taste blood were all she remembered before her world turned black.

Chapter 2

Of all the things Lexi thought she would do the week after her twenty-ninth birthday, returning to Silverton wasn't even on the list. It wasn't that she didn't return home once in a while to visit, she had. This time was different because she was saying good-bye to her nana.

Lexi's grandmother had been fighting a losing battle against liver cancer for a while. Although she missed her terribly, she wouldn't want that life for her if she were to stay. Towards the end, she was a frail shell of the strong woman who helped raise her. A humble and stubborn woman who worked for everything she had, was destroyed by an illness that forced her pride aside while others tended to what she thought was her responsibility.

She wiped a stray tear that fell down her cheek as she drove her BMW down Route 86 towards the city limits. After she graduated high school, she attended NYU where she completed her degree in Criminal Science before entering Law School through Stanford. She was immediately offered a job as legal counsel for the District Attorney's office and she loved her job immensely.

After the accident, she stayed in Houston to complete rehab. She spent her last summer before going to College rushed from doctors, physiotherapists, and psychologists' appointments. All the medicine in the world wouldn't take away the scars, the physical and emotional. She visited occasionally as Nana became sick and to visit her parents, but she never stayed long enough to get comfortable. Her father tried constantly to get her to work with him at his firm as a partner, but she couldn't stomach the idea of setting down roots in a place that only reminded her of heartache.

The phone rang, indicating a call

from her mother and she quickly pushed the answer button on her steering wheel.

"Hey, mom! I'm still driving but I should reach home in about fifteen minutes."

"Oh dear, I'm so glad you're close because I was starting to pace with excitement. I've prepared a special family meal for your return! I'll see you shortly, Lex! Love you!" she said before she made kissing sounds into the phone and hung up.

Jessica Scott was always the type of mother who doted on her children. She literally would smoother them in affection and did so many times despite their protests. She had a kind heart, but she hated that Lexi chose to stay in New York after graduating rather than return to Silverton. But she had Jack to pester since he decided to stay and needed far more guidance than she did. Jack never grew out of his frat boy days and still spent a lot of time partying and picking up girls.

She drove past the "Welcome to Silverton! Home of the state's best apple pie" sign. Dolly's warm crisp apple pie passed through her mind and her stomach rumbled in protest for her neglect. Silverton had changed in the past ten years. Shopfronts that were previously abandoned had been restored into new, such as the pastry shop, a bar called the Barn House - or Bar Hoe, she wasn't sure — and some additional retail stores. Main Street was decorated with beautiful flowers and iron streetlamps that looked like something out of a Broadway musical.

She pulled into a parking spot in front of the pastry shop called "Buns of Steel". The shop had a quaint eclectic vibe with the large bay window displaying various cakes, cupcakes, and desserts, that was flourished with sprinkles and glitter. It stood out from the rest of the stores since the shop was bright pink on the outside, while every other store stayed a muted white with red brick.

Lexi breathed deep and exhaled, praying that she didn't bump into anyone while she was there. She forced herself to exit her car and walked into the shop. A vintage gold plated bell above the door signalled her arrival. The inside was just as unique as the outside, with plush pink leather booths, black and white photos of celebrities eating a cake or other desserts, and mini lights strung from the rafters.

Lexi moved towards the counter, where a light-haired woman was standing with her back turned away from Lexi as she prepared something for the glass display case. She eyed the pastries when she turned to greet her. Shock descended on her face and Lexi's heart dropped to her heels as she recognized those piercing blue eyes.

Valerie.

Lexi began to fidget. She turned her back on everything and everyone when she left Silverton ten years ago and despite Val's attempts to keep in touch, Lexi found it hard to hear about things back home. Especially since Valerie, Brett and Sawyer had been fused at the hip that summer. Valerie hid the brief expression of shock and quickly adjusted to a sweet smile as she flipped the switch on recognition.

"What can I get for you?" she asked.

Lexi's heart broke into a million

pieces for the friendship she gave up on all those years ago. Lexi knew that her appearance hadn't changed enough for her childhood friend not to recognize her. Valerie was hurt and Lexi wasn't planning to stay, so why make things more awkward than they needed to be.

"Can I get the lemon meringue pie, please?"

Valerie nodded and moved about to prepare her order, while Lexi pressed her debit card to the machine. Valerie handed over the pie, perfectly boxed with a bright pink bow, before offering a dismissal.

"Here you go. Have a good day," Valerie said overly sweetly, and in a blink, she had speed-walked to a back room and out of Lexi's sight. Lexi sighed as she exited the store. God, she was such a dick. She should have kept in touch with Valerie. She should have visited her the other times she came to town, but she didn't want to have to talk to her about Sawyer. About losing her virginity to him and how he had said cruel words behind her back to his friends.

Steeling herself, she continued her

drive back to her family home which, sat on a beautiful acre of land on the upper east side of Silverton. The lawn was perfectly landscaped to accentuate the colonel two storey with two large pillars bracing the stairs and front porch. She loved her family home and she had so many wonderful memories from her childhood there. The place was every bit a part of her as those memories that she held in her heart.

Stepping out of the car she breathed in the lilacs and fresh-cut grass, as she removed her suitcase from the back seat. The front door of the house opened and her father rushed out to help her lift her suitcase. Always a southern gentleman, Baxter Scott was a jovial man who took pride in maintaining a healthy lifestyle. His once dark brown hair was peppered with silver but otherwise, he still resembled the upstanding father who attended all her debate team tournaments. His large arms wrapped around Lexi as he greeted her on the stone walkway to the home.

"Hello, peanut!" He'd always called her peanut and something about the nickname melted her heart. To her parents, she would never be a disappointment and their love was unconditional. Lexi embraced her father in a tight hug and caught his unique scent of Old Spice and gun oil.

"Hello daddy. I missed you."

He pulled her back and held her out to assess her. "Peanut, you look far too skinny. Your mama is going to serve you three-course meals the whole time you're here," he chuckled, as they walked inside the house.

"There she is!" a deep booming voice filled the foyer before Lexi was swept up into big arms. She laughed as she always did when her brother greeted her. He never missed an opportunity to remind her how small she was compared to him. He set her down still laughing before planting a kiss on his cheek.

Jack took after their mother, with his light brown hair, chocolate-colored eyes, strong square facial features, all topped off with muscles that seemed to multiply every time she saw him.

"Hey Munchkin!" she greeted him.

"You know I'm three times the size of you now, Lex," he smiled. She patted his cheek tauntingly.

"You may beef yourself up, Munch-kin but you'll always be my baby brother," he groaned, as she chuckled. It was so easy to rile him up. She heard pots and pans fighting in the kitchen and already knew where her mother was spending her day.

She took a moment to appreciate the foyer, where a long oak banister paired with the stairs to the second floor. Family photos lined the wall as she walked to her childhood bedroom. Every smile and laugh captured in a snapshot of time on display. It was no coincidence that there were no photos of her after the accident. She had never felt comfortable with her body after-ward.

She turned the crystal doorknob and swung open her bedroom door. Her four-poster queen size bed was still covered with her purple bedspread. Posters covered her walls of the Backstreet Boys and N'Sync. Strings of mini lights were tied around the canopy that draped over her bed. The bay window seat was covered with her stuffed animals and Beanie Babies and she ran her fingers along the two bookshelves on either side of the window. Her classical favorites front and center, their spines and pages showed signs of frequent use.

"I hope you plan to spend some time at home during this visit," her mother's voice called from the doorway. She was covered in flour with a checkered apron that wrapped around her tiny waist and her long chestnut hair pulled back in a frazzled ponytail.

"Mama, I'd give you a hug but it looks like you just lost a fight to a bag of flour," Lexi teased, as she reached in to kiss her mother on the cheek. Her mother laughed and it was a sound that was warm and comforting like she wrapped her arms around her in a hug only a mother could give.

"Well, I've been busy making pies for the church bake sale this weekend. It's been hell trying to keep Jack and your dad from stealing one or two for themselves."

"Do you want some help?" Lexi asked. Her mother waved her hand dismissively.

"Goodness no… You've had a long drive, get settled and we'll talk more during dinner. Which will be served promptly at six pm," she ordered.

With that, she turned on her heel and gracefully pranced down the stairs to yell at Jack for taking advantage of her being upstairs to steal a piece of a pie. Laughing, Lexi turned to her childhood bedroom and reveled in all the good and bad memories it held.

It was going to be a long visit.

Chapter 3

SAWYER

"Morning to my number one lady!" Sawyer drawled, as he leaned into kiss Miss Martha on the cheek. Miss Martha had been a staple in their family since Sawyer and Remi were little and she was a damn fine cook.

"Now, now, brother dearest I may get very jealous," Aubrey taunted, as she entered the back door rushing to give him and Miss Martha a kiss on the cheek before she poured herself a cup of coffee.

Aubrey and Remi had a place down by the lake, but she still visited every other morning to take advantage of Miss Martha's cooking. Aubrey and Remi married a couple of months ago at the beginning of June in a quiet ceremony. His brother had never been happier and Aubrey kicks his ass so he doesn't have to do it. She was the yin to his yang and he was hopelessly in love with her.

"Oh, darling... you know there is plenty of Sawyer to go around," he tossed her a saucy wink.

"Only a douchbag talks about himself in the third person, Sawyer," Remi said, as he leaned in to kiss his wife. Sawyer's phone rang and he sighed. Time to get back to daily life as the Sheriff. At twenty-nine years old, Sawyer was the youngest Sheriff to be elected into the position. An accomplishment he took great pride in.

"Duty calls y'all," he said, to the crowd gathered in the kitchen and grabbed a blueberry muffin and travel mug before he picked up his phone and headed to his cruiser.

"McGuire," he answered.

"Hey Sheriff, it's Parker I think you're going to want to get down to the office," Parker said quietly. Parker rarely called him with this type of request. Immediately red flags started blowing.

"What's going on Parker? I don't like being sideswiped before I've had my morning coffee," he allowed the phone to connect to Bluetooth before peeling out of the drive.

"W-Well sir, a young man was arrested overnight vandalizing several businesses on Main street... and uh," he stammered. Parker's resistance didn't sit well with him.

"Spit it out Deputy," he snipped.

"S-Sir, the young man is your nephew. Jordan is on her way but I suspect she'll want to speak with you."

"God damn it, Leo! I'll be there in five minutes Parker," he barked before he hung up the phone and he ran his hand over his face.

It was too early in the morning to be dealing with that shit. Leo had been struggling since Jordan informed him of the plan for adoption. Leo's mother consented to have her parental rights stripped, but Leo continued to hold out hope for her. Rather than settling into his life, he pushed Jordan to her limits and this was the icing on the cake.

Sawyer parked in his spot in front of the office and spied Jordan walking towards him. Ah, shit… She was beyond pissed and he could tell just from the death to everyone look on her face.

"Jordan, I need you to stay calm right now," he prompted, as she joined him to walk into the office.

"Did you seriously just tell me to stay calm. In the twenty-nine years, you've known me has telling me to stay calm ever worked?" she asked, as she followed him into his office and slammed the door behind her. He already felt a headache coming and it wasn't even nine am.

He sat in his leather chair and eyed the stack of paperwork mounting on his desk. "Jordan, I will talk with him and the prosecutor, but this isn't the first charge he has had and I suspect they'll want to make an example out of him. Let me get the details and find out when he's due to appear in court. In the meantime, you might want to get a lawyer for him."

She dropped into the chair in front

of his desk, shoulders slumped and tears filled up in her beautiful jade eyes. Dark circles had taken residency under those eyes and he could tell she'd been worrying more often as the crease in between her brows was deeper.

"Sawyer, I'm at a loss. I don't know how to help him. He won't let me in and it's killing me to see him self-destruct this way." She ran her fingers across her cheeks to catch the free tears.

Sawyer rounded the desk and took her in his arms. It was hard to see his strong and resilient sister falling apart. She sobbed into his chest and he kissed the top of her head before pulling back and meeting her gaze.

"I'll do what I can Jo Jo. Do you know any lawyers you can call?" he asked softly.

"The court-appointed one has already dealt with Leo before and it's clear he has no interest in fighting for him. He's already typed him as a lost cause. I'll make some calls and see if I can find another more appropriate while he's waiting."

He nodded and moved to leave the

office, "Stay as long as you need, but I'm going to speak with him."

He stepped out of the office and found Parker to get the full report on what happened. Parker was sitting at his desk and rose as Sawyer's steps approached.

"Sir, here's the report, you may want to look it over before you go talk to him," Parker handed him the file with a serious expression.

Sawyer reviewed the complaint and the charges. Criminal trespassing, vandalism, destruction of property, resisting arrest, and ...possession? What the fuck? Sawyer looked up at Parker from the top of the file.

"What are you not telling me, Parker?"

"Sir, Leo was doing more than spray painting penises on storefronts. He appeared under the influence of something according to the arresting deputy and he put up a struggle. He took a swing at Collins and when they frisked him they found a small baggy of marijuana."

Sawyer's hand immediately went to

the bridge of his nose as he felt the migraine increase pressure behind his eyes. He was going to kill him. There was no way he would make it out of those charges freely.

"For your own safety Parker, do not speak to Jordan about this. Don't even make eye contact, got it? She's medusa today because she will turn you to stone if she hears anything she doesn't want to hear."

"Yes, sir," Parker nodded.

Sawyer entered the holding cells and spotted Leo laying on the hard as nails cot. It was a good thing there was a wall of bars between them right now. His eyes were closed and it looked like he was sleeping. This kid. Using his flashlight, Sawyer wasted no time banging on the bars starling his nephew and caused him to fall on his ass.

"What the fuck?" he shouted before he turned and realized who he was talking with. "Shit, Sawyer... Listen, I'm really sorry and I've done the time. Can you please get me out of this hellhole?" he pleads.

What a sense of entitlement the punk had if he thought he was going to walk away from this. Sawyer leaned on the wall and crossed his arms over his broad chest.

"Here's the thing Leo, there's nothing I can do to help you weasel your way out of this. You're a minor but the prosecutor could ask to try you as an adult given that this isn't your first infraction."

"W-What do you mean? I'm a child!" he screamed.

"You are a child. A child making a terrible decision and causing the adults in his life who love him to go through hell. I have a crying, stressed out sister in my office because of your poor decisions. How would you feel if it was Emma who was distraught and upset?"

His face fell and softened at the mention of his little sister. He may very well be a little shit, but he would do anything for that little girl.

"I never thought about that," he mumbled, as he ran his hands through his hair.

"Where did you get the drugs?" Sawyer asked, "Was it yours? Are you using?"

"No! No, I was drinking last night but

I swear I wasn't smoking anything. I was holding on to it for a friend."

"Oh c'mon Leo! Who are you trying to fool here? That's the oldest excuse in the book," he bellowed.

"I know... what happens next?"

"Well, Jordan is working on getting you a lawyer before you have to appear in front of the judge. Hopefully, you'll be released into her care while the lawyers do their jobs. In the meantime, make yourself comfortable because if you don't get released, you'll be heading to juvenile detention," he said, as he headed towards the door.

"I'm sorry," Leo mumbled. Sawyer turned to face him.

"I'm not the one you need to be apologizing to right now. No matter how hard you push us away Leo, we will be there, whether you like that or not. You are part of our family, adoption or not."

Sawyer made his way to his office to speak with Jordan but stopped when the prosecutor grabbed his attention. Colin Kincaid always had a grudge against the

McGuires for reasons no one knew. Colin was as slimy and manipulative as they came. He gave lawyers a bad name because he was just a creep.

"Kincaid," Sawyer nodded.

"McGuire. It seems one of yours has found their way into the cells again," he smirked, and Sawyer mentally envisioned beating the living shit out of him. That little comment warranted a solid right hook.

"I think we'll push to try him as an adult, given his history," Colin examined his nails, as though he had better things to do with his time.

An uppercut for that comment.

"Now, now Kincaid it would seem unfair to judge a teenager for their history. If anyone should understand that, it should be you. As I recall, daddy bailed you out of many an incident," Sawyer smiled sweetly. The bastard could fly to fuck.

He scowled and moved closer to Sawyer as if trying to intimidate him. Sawyer had several inches on him so, it was useless.

"Tell your sister she better get a good

lawyer, because I'm bringing my game to this one," he sneered, before turning on his heel and exited the office.

He fucking hated that douche bag.

Jordan's still sat in the chair when he returned. She jumped when he entered but immediately demanded answers about Leo. It was time to tell her everything about the charges.

"Jordan... I think you should sit down..." Sawyer prompted, but before he could explain anything her cell phone rang.

"Sorry, I should get this. Jessica from church has contacts in the legal area since her husband is a partner at a legal firm. She said she would call me back."

Jordan stepped out to speak with Jessica before returning with a smile.

"I assume you have good news," he prompted.

"Jessica said her husband doesn't have the ability as he's already filled his pro bono quota, but that their daughter is in town for a bit and would be willing to assist."

Sawyer looked up and noticed that

her smile slipped.

"That sounds like a good thing, Jo Jo. Why do you look like someone popped all the heads off your barbies?" he recalled, how pissed she was when Remi did that when they were younger. He also hid the heads in different spots around the ranch. Pretty sure there were still some missing.

"Their daughter..." she hesitated.

"The lawyer..." Sawyer prompted.

Jordan grimaced and then unleashed her news. It's Lexi Scott, Sawyer."

His heart skipped a beat and feelings he had been trying to keep buried began to surface. Lexi was back in town.

Could things get any worse?

Chapter 4

LEXI

"Lexi!" her mother called out, from the bottom of the stairs. Lexi had never been a morning person, so when her mother's yell is the first thing she hears, it made for a bad day. Lexi jumped up out of the bed, mascara turned her eyes black and her hair was matted in the back.

Lexi rubbed her hand across her chin to wipe away the drool she was sporting before she slipped her feet into her old rabbit slippers.

"Coming!" she bellowed in return as she pulled on her Hello Kitty bathrobe and made her way downstairs. She scuffed her way into the kitchen where her parents have gathered. She rubbed her eyes and made her way to the coffee maker when her mother speaks.

"There she is! Oh, peanut... We figured you would have been up by now," her mother motioned her, towards the living room and grabbed her coffee. Thus, ensuring she follows. She needed her coffee in the morning to function.

"Mama, you know I'm not a morning person and why aren't we drinking coffee in the kitchen like normal?" she whined.

"Peanut, please come in. I'd like you to meet someone," her dad eyed her state of inappropriate meeting attire.

"Daddy, no one said anything about meeting someone. I'm nowhere near appropriate for human sight right now."

Her father chuckled, "I'm sure Jordan won't mind considering it's a special circumstance. Come."

Lexi sipped her coffee and followed her father into the family room where a striking woman sat on their sofa, drinking a cup of coffee. She was tall with jade green eyes and light brown hair. She was a beautiful woman and is dressed professionally. The irony of their appearances is not lost on her. Jordan stood when Lexi entered the room and offered her hand to shake, which she accepted tentatively.

"I'm Doctor Jordan McGuire. I'm a family friend of your parents."

"I'm Lexi... the Scott family morning grump" she joked. Jordan smiled at her lame joke about her appearance.

"Lexi, please have a seat," her father asked.
They sat in the living room of her mother's unique decorating styles. Who knew there were so many different shades of white?

"Lexi," her father started, "Jordan here has been fostering two children for a couple of years now. Emma is six and Leo is thirteen. She's in the process of adopting them." He smiled at Jordan and Lexi's respect for the woman skyrocketed. It took a special person to care for children who had trauma in their backgrounds.

"My eldest, Leo, has been struggling with the idea of adoption and has put our family through the wringer. He's been in trouble with the law a time or two, but last night he was arrested while spray painting all the storefronts on Main Street. He also has several other charges," Jordan added.

"Has he been appointed a court-mandated lawyer?" Lexi asked.

"He had used the mandated lawyer before, but honestly, we didn't feel that he wanted to fight for Leo. And right now, he needs someone who will be able to fight for him."

Lexi shook her head in confusion, "I don't understand what this has to do with me?"

"Lexi I'd like for you to attend his first appearance as a favor to Jordan. Right now Leo is still locked up and they'd like for him to be released into the custody of his family pending trial," her father said.

"Okay. But Dad you know that I'm only here for a couple of weeks. Once Nana's will reading is settled, I'll be making my way back to New York," she countered. "I have no issue assisting right now, but I won't be here for the trial."

"We know that, but until I can assign the file to someone at the firm I thought you would be the best option. I also took into consideration that the prosecutor is Colin Kincaid and I want someone who can match his ability in the courtroom. I don't doubt that he will want to make an example of Leo," he said.

Her father had always been passionate about fighting for the underdog and Leo certainly seemed to have experienced enough in his short lifetime.

"Ok. When's the bail hearing?" Lexi asked.

"This afternoon at two pm," Jordan advised.

Standing, Lexi laid her empty cup on the table and nodded at her father. "I guess I should go get dressed. I'll want to meet with Leo before the court this afternoon, speak with the arresting officer, his social worker, and the prosecutor to see what we can do about some of those charges," she confirmed.

Tears filled Jordan's eyes as she grabbed Lexi and pulled her into a hug. Lexi wasn't accustomed to her clients hugging her and she awkwardly patted her back.

"I'll wait for you and we can go together. The clinic is closed today so I can deal with this family matter," Jordan admitted.

Lexi ran upstairs and took a quick shower before she opened her suitcase and whipped out a navy pencil skirt, ivory silk blouse, and matching blazer. She slipped her feet into her nude heels and pulled her hair back in a high bun. She applied a little makeup, but unfortunately, there was nothing she could do about the long jagged scar that ran from the crown of her head and along the side of her face. For a while, she tried to cover the scar with her hair so people wouldn't stare at her. But now, she didn't give a crap. Everyone in Silverton knew of her accident, but she didn't return afterward to face the town. She grabbed her purse and made her way to the foyer where Jordan was waiting.

"Thank you for helping. It's really such a relief," she exclaimed.

"It's the least I can do. Shall we?" Lexi moved over to her parents and gave them both a kiss before heading out.

"Thank you, Peanut," her father

whispered. She smiled and nodded as she left the house with Jordan. They climbed into her BMW and Lexi had to appreciate her choice of car.

"So, Lexi... how long has it been since you've been in Silverton?" she asked. Jordan's attempt at small talk was typical and the reason she hated interacting with others when she visited home.

"I've been gone for about ten years. I left right after high school for NYU. Then moved to attend Law School at Stanford," she answered pointedly and with as little detail as possible.

"Have you been back to visit?"

"Yeah, on holidays and special occasions. I visited just last month with Nana passed away. I'm visiting now because her will is being read tomorrow and I was required to be present."

They pulled up in front of the Sheriff's office and Lexi assured Jordan that she could manage from there, leaving her in the hall to wait. Lexi climbed the stairs to the Sheriff's office and stopped at the reception desk where a young deputy sat. She approached and quickly fixed her expression to be all business. The deputy's gaze flicked to her and then did a double-take.

"Hello. I'm the attorney Leo McGuire. I would like to speak with my client and the arresting officer."

The deputy was adorable with his boyish features and had an innocent dumbfounded look on his face. She could eat him for breakfast.

"Um, sure thing. I'll have the Sheriff come to speak with you," he said tentatively.

"I'd like to see my client first as he has a hearing in less than three hours and I have many things to accomplish before then," she challenged. Lexi moved around the desk and made her way towards, what she assumed was the holding cells. She looked at the young buck's name tag.

"Deputy Johnson is it?" he nodded. "Would you please unlock the required doors and provide me access to my client?" she asked. It wasn't a question as much as a demand.

He nodded swiping his key card to

provide her access to the holding cells. There she found a small boy sat on a disgusting cot with his head on his knees.

"Leo?" she asked. His head perked up and he walked towards the bars.

"That's me. Are you the lawyer?".

"I am. My name is Lexi and I'll be attending court this afternoon to discuss your bail. I assume the Sheriff spoke with you about the charges you're facing," she sternly addressed the boy. This shouldn't be a pleasant process for anyone, but especially someone so young and impressionable.

"Yes ma'am," he pulled his gaze to his shoes.

"Do you deny the allegations?"

"No, ma'am."

"Are you willing to do whatever is required of you by the court to rectify your error?"

"Yes, ma'am."

"Good, I'll see what I can do about getting you out of here. But rest assured Leo, this isn't going away so if you are released, I need you to keep your ass on the straight and narrow, you get me?" she drew his gaze to hers as she wanted him to understand that this was real life and there are consequences for every action. Something she learned the hard way and had the physical scars to prove it.

"Yes, ma'am," he mumbled.

"Fine. Now, I'll go see what I can do," she said turning on her heels and moving out of the holding cells and was greeted by Deputy Johnson. She smiled politely.

"Can you provide me a copy of the police report for this case? And I will need to speak with the Sheriff."

"I can get you the report, no problem. But I believe the Sheriff may be... ah... indisposed at the moment," he said, his eyes hit the floor. Laughter was heard from behind the door which indicated the Sheriff's office in bold gold lettering. Lexi's brow rose and Johnson seemed to know what she was thinking. She moved swiftly and knocked on the door firmly.

"I'm in the middle of something..." a deep voice announced, followed by a female giggle. If this dickhead thought that he can get laid on the job, he had another thing coming. She was on a tight timeline and couldn't wait for him to whack off to get what she needed. She knocked again, louder.

"Go away," the voice replied. Okay, she was done being professional, now she was royally pissed. How dare this asshat take advantage of his position of authority. Who the fuck did he think he was?

She twisted the doorknob and barged into the office. Straddled on the man's lap on a leather couch was a petite blond who wore a tight pink mini skirt and tube top. Her blond hair was not natural and Lexi was certain there were many things about the woman that wasn't natural. All she saw of the Sheriff was his legs.

"What the heck, Parker?" he bellowed.

"Not Parker and certainly not pleased to know that an elected official is using his office for some afternoon delight. So if you're done doing whatever inappropriate thing you were doing, I'd like to get on with my day. And my day can't move forward until I have had the unfortunate pleasure of a conversation with you. So, if Candy could move along that would be great," she said sternly. Lexi's blood pressure was rising with this jackass and her hands are fisted and placed on her hips in her Wonder Woman pose.

"My name is Mandy... not Candy," Blondie whined, before rising and grabbing her purse. She flicked her hair as she made her way out the door. Lexi watched her as she left and questioned whether or not she needed to be tested for STIs just from being in her presence.

"Last I was aware, having a lunch break is not against the law and nor did I provide you permission to enter the office..." he clipped. His back was turned to her so she still couldn't see his face.

"Well, I have a scared thirteen-year-old boy locked up that I need to get bailed out, so if we could move this along it would be great. I don't have time to wait for you to have a booty call while I'm trying to work," she snarled. The jackass was trying her last nerve.

Then he turned and her heart dropped as their eyes met and a flash of recognition crossed his stupidly handsome face. A face that haunted her dreams and made her blood run cold.

"Lexi?" he asked seemingly surprised. He stood immobile when he recognized her.

Flashes of the night that changed her life flicked across her vision and her chest tightened and the air left her lungs. *Not now Lexi. Not now.* She couldn't have an anxiety attack right now.

She took a deep breath before talking. She was not going to let him get to her. She was not seventeen years old anymore. She was not weak or easily intimidated.

"Hello, Sawyer. If you don't mind, I'd like to get some information before Leo is seen this afternoon," she said, fixing her expression to show no emotional response whatsoever to the man who stole her virginity and dismissed her like trash. That night changed her life.

"Of course. It's ... nice to see you. How long has it been? Nine years?" he walked towards his desk, pulled out Leo's file and handed it to her.

"Ten actually," she corrected.

He rubbed the back of his neck before he met her gaze again, "So, you're going to represent Leo?"

"I believe we already covered that," she responded coldly, while she skimmed through the file in her hands. She gathered that her client had a criminal record and that it was likely the prosecutor wanted to set an example of him.

"Yes, well... Leo is my nephew."

"I'm aware. Your sister drove me here and I'm doing this as a favor to her on behalf of my family. I'll seek for Leo to be released into her custody while a trial or plea bargain is settled," she said drily.

"That would be best. He's a good kid, he just makes stupid mistakes. But I guess we all did at his age," he smiled. She didn't.

"Stupid mistakes can often mean life and death for many people, Sheriff. The goal is to prevent him from re-offending before something like that happens."

He stared at her for a long time and

she knew that he was looking at her scar.

"Maybe while you're in town we can get together for a drink, maybe catch up?"

Did he just ask her out? Like they were friends? Was he so stupid that he thought that was what was happening here?

"Absolutely not," she said, angrily before she turned on her heel and headed for the door. His hand caught her elbow and she flinched away from his touch, but still aware of how his touch lit her up inside.

"Why not?" he asked, "You married or in a relationship?" He sought out her hands to look for a ring.

"No, I'm not. You're just the last person in this galaxy I would ever want to share anything with," she admitted, as his mouth popped open and hung in shock. He was not used to women rejecting him.

Tough shit.

With that said, she turned and exited the office heading to the prosecutor's office to distract her from Sawyer fucking McGuire.

Chapter 5

SAWYER

"What the fuck just happened?" Sawyer mumbled to himself, as he watched Lexi Scott leave his office.

She just blatantly rejected him. Sawyer didn't have too large of an ego to say that women didn't reject him. But, he didn't know what he did to cause such a disgusted reaction. He recalled the night they were intimate. He was such a dick. Part of him had been in love with Lexi since middle school. He was honest when he told her he wouldn't push her into anything. If she had pulled back, he would have walked away with his pride.

After her accident, he visited her in the hospital every day. She wasn't conscious for most of his visits, and when she did wake, she was on a large cocktail of medications that left her drowsy. He was not sure she remembered any of their visits. That night changed her life, but it also changed his. He realized that night that he needed to treat people better and that he needed to be a better person. It was why he joined the US Army and then moved into law enforcement when he left the service. He tried to repent for his poor behavior.

A knock on his office door pulled him from his deep thoughts. He looked towards the newest distraction and found Brett. After all the years that passed, Brett and Sawyer still had a good relationship.

Brett didn't look a day over twenty-five and he worked as a contractor in town, with a specialty in restoration. The man had a gift and his eye for design was well known all across the state. He fell in love with Lucy in college and they had Sara, who was now six years old. Lucy was diagnosed with stage four breast Cancer when Sara was two years old. She did treatments and surgeries, but in the end, it wasn't successful. She passed away three years ago and no one has turned Brett's head since. He'd rather spend his Friday night curled up with Sara watching Monster's Inc for the five-hundredth time than be at the Barn House with him.

"Hey man, did I just see, not one, but two pissed off women leave your office?" Brett snickered. He entered Sawyer's office and sprawled out on his leather couch, where Sawyer had planned to relieve some stress with Mandy minutes ago.

"You sure did," Sawyer groaned. He placed his hands behind his head and rested his feet on his desk.

Brett still wore his gear from his renovation job down at Halley's B & B, leaving a trail of dust and dirt on his couch and floor.

"I know the first is Mandy, but who's the other woman?" Brett asked.

"Lexi Scott," Sawyer admitted. Brett's face scrunched in confusion as he struggled to make the connection.

"What the heck is she doing in your office?" he asked.

"Leo got into some more trouble last night and Jordan called in a favor with the family. Lexi's a lawyer and she's visiting," he huffed.

Brett whistled as his eyebrows found themselves lodged in his hairline. "Well, you do remember the night of her accident, right?" he asked.

"Of course I do," he snapped. In reality, he hadn't forgiven himself for how he treated Lexi. He'd been stupid and inconsiderate.

"You know her grandmother passed recently. I'm guessing she's only in town for a little while before she takes off back to the big apple," Brett said.

"Probably for the best, she didn't exactly give me the warm and cozy feeling," he admitted.

"Might have something to do with the stripper visiting you when you're on the clock," Brett scoffed.

"Maybe, but I've always loved the company of a woman, Brett. And I've never been shy about it."

"Speaking of the ladies in our lives, Sara is wondering when her Godfather is planning to stop by again. She and Mr.

Bunny have been talking non-stop about the new tiara she has for Uncle Sawyer," Brett smiled. He knew there was nothing Sawyer wouldn't do for Sara.

Sawyer ran his fingers through his hair, "You know, I've been thinking I need to spice things up with a bit of bling. How's about Friday?" he asked. Brett nodded and stood to exit his office but turned to face Sawyer. His expression was no longer fun and amused.

"Watch yourself around Lex. You maybe my best friend, but I will kick your ass if you fuck with her the way you did back in high school," he threatened. Sawyer nodded because he already knew that he deserved to have his ass kicked if he treated a woman like that again.

That night changed Lexi, without a doubt. But it also changed him in ways that he couldn't even begin to acknowledge. He pushed aside his thoughts about Lexi and moved to get to Leo's hearing. He had Parker transport him to the courthouse and he'd planned to meet Jordan there.

When he arrived outside the courthouse, he had the unfortunate luck to bump into Colin Kincaid. The pretentious dick leaned against his Lexus with his brand name aviators. Just laying eyes on the fucker boiled his blood. He took responsibility for his role in what happened with Lexi all those years ago, but that dick never even as much as acknowledging what happened to her.

Sawyer got out of his car and walked towards the courthouse with intentions of ignoring Colin. Unfortunately, he had a different idea and popped out in front of him to goad him some more about Leo being arrested.

"Well, hello Sheriff. Coming to support your kin and their bad habits?" he snarled with a twisted grin on his douche bag face. Sawyer mentally ran through all the ways he could hide his body before he spoke.

"Get out of my way, Kincaid," Sawyer growled trying hard to hold onto any rational thought.

"I guess the apple doesn't fall too far from the tree, right? Makes sense the boy would be a druggie like his mother..."

"Mr. Kincaid," a strong feminine voice came from behind Sawyer. "I would hope that your opinions of my client will not impede your ability to be professional. Otherwise, I would ask that you recuse yourself from this case so that the law can do its job," Lexi challenged.

Sawyer looked to his side and saw Lexi, standing strong with her head held high and a fierce stare glared directly at Kincaid. Kincaid eyed her up and down but didn't recognize her until she turned her face and her scar was on full display.

"Lexi Scott?" he sounded surprised.

"Yes, and based on what I've over-heard of this conversation, I could argue that you're unable to be unbiased and pro-ceed based on facts of this case," she con-tinued.

"Well, L-Lexi," Kincaid stuttered.

"Ms. Scott will work just fine. And be-fore we go in front of the judge perhaps we should speak privately about what is best for my client. I would truly hate to have to discuss with the judge my concerns around the prosecution's bias," she nodded towards Sawyer, who couldn't wipe the grin off his face, "Sheriff," she said in acknowledgment.

"Ms. Scott," he grinned.

Poor Kincaid's face was white as a sheet as Lexi grabbed him by the arm and escorted him to a briefing room to discuss the case.

"Sawyer!" Jordan called from up the sidewalk. She was flanked by the whole God damn family, Aubrey, Remi, and Daisy.

"Jordan, I'll take you to see Lexi. She's speaking with Kincaid right now. From the little I've seen of her, she's a shark and is probably going to eat Kincaid for lunch," he assured.

"Oh, thank God she's here," Jordan said, as relief passed through her body and her shoulders relaxed. "Let's go."

They ascended the stairs and made their way into the courthouse hallway where the briefing rooms were situated. Kincaid left one room and appeared red and flustered. Good, that meant Lexi was doing what she could for Leo. Shortly after, Lexi exited the room and spotted Jordan.

"Jordan, can we speak?" she asked.

"Of course," Jordan replied.

"Sheriff?" Lexi asked.

"Yes, Ms. Scott," he answered.

"I'd like to confer with my client before we are called into court. Can you please have him brought to me?" she posed, and he nodded in agreement.

He descended the stairwell to the holding cells located in the basement. Leo was there, secluded from the others of course. Being a child, placing him in the same cells as the adults would be suicide.

"Leo," he called opening the cell doors.

"Is it time?" Leo questioned.

"Not yet, but your lawyer wants to speak with you. Hands behind your back," Sawyer directed. Leo was surprised by the request and Sawyer leaned into him.

"Son, you don't want special treatment around here, trust me. You don't want to stand out among the rest, you get me?" he whispered, and Leo nodded his understanding.   Sawyer handcuffed him and escorted him like any other prisoner.

When he brought him into the room, Jordan leaped to her feet and rushed to hug him. She pulled back and looked him over as if assessing him for injuries.

"Can we sit please?" Lexi asked.

Everyone took a seat, Lexi on one side of the table and the McGuires on the other. Leo sat in between Jordan and Sawyer.

"Firstly, I need to advise that I typically would only speak with my client, but given he is a minor, his guardian shall be present. Sheriff, I know you're family, but you're also the law. I'm asking you to leave this conversation as required under client privilege," she said flatly.

She asked him to leave. She had to be out of her mind if she thought that he was not going to be present for things concerning his family.

"I'm not leaving," Sawyer rebutted.

"Yes, Sheriff, you are and you will. You're not just family in this situation and I am not going to risk his privacy by having you present. Nor do I want to give Kincaid any more ammunition to fire at us in open court. Now, you can leave of your own accord, which I would strongly recommend. Or I can have the court officers escort you from this meeting room. Whatever you chose will be fine by me," she said, as cold as a fall morning breeze.

Sawyer glared at the woman who'd been entrusted to represent Leo with shock and a little bit of respect. As much as he wanted to argue with her, he had enough sense to know that they were wasting valuable time.

"Fine," he gritted before he stood and exited the meeting room. He paced the hallway in front of the office for what seemed like hours, but in reality, it was fifteen minutes max. When the door finally opened, Jordan greeted him.

"What's happening, JoJo?" he asked.

"Lexi thinks that prosecution is firm on moving forward with the charges, but she's going to try and get him released into my custody," she said her voice little and defeated.

He grabbed her and pulled her into a hug, hoping to provide some comfort to her. He didn't know how to fix it for her and the brother in him always wanted to fix what was hurting her. This was the one time where he wanted to value his role as a brother over the role of the Sheriff.

The court was called and the family made their way into the courtroom while Lexi strutted in with an officer and Leo. She was stunning in her pencil skirt, heels and blazer. Her hair pulled up in a tight bun on top of her head, but wisps of hair had come loose and dangled along her face. The confidence she had in the courtroom told him that she was in her element. This was her world and she ruled it with an iron fist. There was a slight flush to her cheeks and a glimmer in her eyes that added to her beauty. She was beautiful as a teenager, but now, she was a woman. She was confident, self-assured, strong and sexy. And fuck if his dick didn't choose that moment to appreciate her.

Lexi approached the desk and stood with Leo, while Kincaid sneered from the opposite side of the room.

"All rise, the honorable Justice

McGraw presiding," the bailiff announced.

A middle-aged woman entered the courtroom and everyone remained silent as she approached the bench.

"You may be seated," the bailiff ordered.

The bailiff called the case to order and Kincaid opened for the prosecution. Sawyer physically grabbed the seat under him to prevent him from yelling profanities at the dick.

"Your honor, we are here today concerning Leo Jennings, who is a minor in the custody of Dr. Jordan McGuire. He has a history of offenses as a minor which includes trespassing and vandalism. He's a repeat offender and has already demonstrated non-compliance with the orders of this court. The prosecution is requesting that he be remanded to the juvenile correctional center until his trial. At which time, the prosecution is requesting that consideration be given to try him as an adult," his harsh baritone rang out in the courtroom.

Sawyer heard Jordan's breathing become strained and he reached a handout to her. She clutched it and squeezed trying to anchor herself to someone.

"Thank you, Mr. Kincaid," the judge nodded and raised her eyes over her glasses. Sawyer felt the scrutiny of Justice McGraw's criticism before and he knew she was all for teaching young people the hard truth early in their criminal behavior.

"Ms. Scott, I must say it is an unexpected pleasure to see you in my courtroom," the judge smiled at Lexi.

Lexi stood before she addressed the court and buttoned over her blazer. "Indeed madam Justice, however, this is an exceptional circumstance," she said moving out from behind the table.

"I would very much like to hear what you have to say on behalf of your client."

"Of course, your Honor. The purpose of today's hearing is to discuss the possibility of bail for Mr. Jennings and despite the lovely introduction Mr. Kincaid has provided on his strategies going forward, these are not the items on the table presently. Mr. Jennings is under the care of Dr. McGuire and she continues to be committed to his care. With that being said, Mr. Jennings is aware that he needs to demonstrate his understanding of the orders in place by this court. He's willing to consent to several conditions to be attached to his bail order," Lexi announced.

Kincaid rose when he heard this proposition.

"Your Honor, with all due respect, Dr. McGuire was unable to control Mr. Jennings or prevent his criminal behavior. I would argue that these added measures would not be sufficient," he said.

"As I'm sure Mr. Kincaid is aware, the last offense was several years ago when Mr. Jennings was in the custody of his mother. This is his first offense since being in the care of Dr. McGuire. I would argue, coun-selor, that Dr. McGuire has provided more than sufficient supervision of Mr. Jennings. Additionally, my client is agreeable to a court-imposed curfew, regular attendance in school and completion of educational programs offered through the youth center in Silverton around criminal behaviors," she boomed.

"Your Honor, this young man is moving down a dark path that could end with someone being seriously injured," Kincaid sneered. Sawyer growled from his seat as he knew that was a dig at Lexi's about the accident.

"Mr. Kincaid may need to revisit law school to relearn the difference between fact and fiction. This is my client's first offense in an extended period, and he has agreed voluntarily to court-imposed conditions on his release. I would argue that these conditions are above what would be expected of any defendant and thus demonstrates his willingness to cooperate," her voice was clipped and agitated.

Kincaid faced Lexi, "Mr. Jennings has had more than enough accommodations, Ms. Scott. Given his connection to the local Sheriff, one may assume that he is being permitted to skirt the limits of the law," he challenged.

"Again counselor, you fail to prove any wrongdoing on behalf of the Sheriff and considering your own opinions about the Sheriff perhaps it would not be wise to cast

THE HEART THE COWBOY BROKE

the first stone. It would be incredibly un-professional if you were unable to maintain an unbiased and harsh attitude towards my client due to your own personal hostil-ities," she snarled back.

"Your client is getting a free ride..."

Lexi interjected, "Are you the right person to talk about getting a free ride, Counsellor?"

The gavel dropped causing a boom-ing sound to echo off the walls. Judge McGraw took off her glasses before she ad-dressed the lawyers in front of her.

"Mr. Kincaid, I hear what you're say-ing, but as Ms. Scott has argued the de-fendant has stipulated to particular condi-tions on his release that will satisfy this court pending further consideration of the charges. Young man please stand," the Judge ordered. Leo stood as Judge McGraw ad-dressed him directly.

"Leo, you have an opportunity be-fore you to demonstrate that you can make changes. I understand that you may be experiencing different challenges, but you need to choose a different path. Should I see you in my courtroom for additional charges, bail will not be granted and I will be inclined to agree with the prosecution. As it stands, I accept the conditions Ms. Scott has put forth but will tell you that should you breach any of those conditions, your bail will be revoked. Do I make myself clear?"

"Yes M-Ma'am," Leo stammered.

"Very well. Ms. Scott, I trust you will draft the order," Judge McGraw asked pointedly.

"Yes, your Honor," Lexi grinned.

The judge left the bench and Jordan wrapped her arms around Lexi as tears filled her eyes. Lexi didn't look comfortable with the physical contact and Sawyer wondered if she had shied away from physical contact since her accident.

Lexi turned to Leo and said, "You heard what I said, Leo. Stay out of trouble or they will throw you in juvie."

She closed her briefcase and briskly strutted past Sawyer without a second glance. Sawyer was caught in the circle of the family who surrounded Leo and was unable to reach her before she left. He wanted to mend some bridges with her for what he did. Or did she know what he did? Did she know he sat by her bedside? Or how it changed him and his path forever?

He needed her to understand.

Of all the women in Sawyer's life, Lexi had always been the one he thought of when he considered settling down. The feelings he had for her in high school were all-consuming, and when she left, he tried to forget about her. But there was something about Lexi Scott that left an impression on his heart and now that she was back in town, he needed to step up his game to get the chance to apologize properly. It was easy to keep his feelings tucked away in the deep dark corners of his heart when she wasn't near. He lost himself in mindless women who never left his feeling anything of any significance. Sure, he'd had relationships, but he never let anyone get close again. Lexi took a piece of his heart with her ten years ago and he never wanted to feel that kind of pain again.

Being so close to her, even temporarily brought old feelings to the surface. She may never forgive him, but he needed to try.

Chapter 6

LEXI

After Lexi settled the hearing for Jordan, she returned to her family home. She was greeted with the sweet smell of strawberries as soon as she opened the door. She suspected that her mother had been in the kitchen most of the day. The woman loved to feed people and people loved her cooking.

Lexi dropped her briefcase in the foyer and followed her nose toward the delicious spread she knew would be waiting. She got to the doorway and eyed the display inside. There was her mother covered head to toe in flour, with a big smile on her face, while she sang along with Deana Carter's *Strawberry Wine*.

"How are you doing there, Mama?"

Lexi asked trying hard to hide the laughter that threatened to slip past her lips.

Her mother turned to Lexi with a sly grin. Daddy loved when Mama baked up a storm in the house. He said it was the reason he married her. She'd been selling her pies at the local church and when Daddy took a bite of her strawberry rhubarb pie, he fell in love.

"Oh, Sugar! You know, maybe you can help me out in the kitchen? I could use a hand and it's been a long time since we made a mess together," her mother requested.

Mama and Lexi spent days in the kitchen baking cupcakes and other wonderful goods around Christmas time. It was a tradition for them and when Nana was around she would join them. They had a wonderful time and it was some of her most cherished memories. She'd be covered head to toe in flour by the end of the afternoon. Tears welled in Lexi's eyes as she remembered those warm memories. This caught her mother's attention and she moved closer to Lexi.

"Lexi, what's wrong? Why are you crying?" she asked wrapping her arms around Lexi in a comforting embrace that unleashed the hurt in her heart.

"Oh, Mama, I was just remembering the good times we had when Nana was around and we baked together," she sniffed.

Her mother pulled back from the embrace and used her hands to wipe away the tears that slid down her cheeks.

"Peanut, Nana knew how much you loved her and she was so proud of you," she said. "Speaking of your grandmother, her lawyer will be coming tonight for supper and afterwards we will hear the will," her mother pulled away and handed her an apron. "Now, how's about we make a mess for Nana?"

Lexi took the apron and joined her mother in the kitchen. She'd forgotten how good it felt to be surrounded by love and family. She missed it. New York was where her dreams came true, but Silverton was where her heart always stayed.

As they prepared dough for a pie they were making, her mother started with the questions about her love life. Honestly, Lexi never saw herself married or with children. It was hard to date in New York due to lack of time, but also, not many people were able to look past the scars on her face. She may get one date, but rarely a second.

"So, how's the big city? Any son-in-law prospects?" her mother asked with a hint of optimism.

"No, Mama, there isn't anyone. I don't have time to date right now, plus... well, you know people don't react well when they see my scars," she sighed.

"Lexi Scott," she turned to face Lexi with her dough covered hands on her hips, "those scars are part of you and as much as I wish I could take that pain for you and carry it myself, I can't. But I will say, if someone doesn't love you for the compassionate, strong, powerful woman that you are, then screw them. They don't deserve you," her mother said firmly.

Her mother had always been the first one to take down people who whispered behind Lexi's back. One Christmas when Lexi had returned home, they had attended church and a social event afterwards. She and her mother had been outside the door when they heard Maddie and Mandy, also known as dumb and dumber, speak about Lexi.

"Can you believe they still allow her in everyday society looking like that?" Mandy had shrieked.

"I know, she should just lock herself in a tower for the rest of her life and save us from the view. Honestly, just looking at her turns my stomach," Maddie countered.

Tears pooled in her eyes as she stood there while they said cruel and horrible things about her. Lexi did not have the strength at the time to stand up for herself, but she watched stunned as her mother moved towards the pair.

"Ladies, I would hope that you are not speaking ill of my daughter," her mother sneered. "Despite the scars that are on her face and body she's still Lexi. And she will always be twice the woman you two could make. Perhaps you two should spend more time in church listening to the good Lord, rather than repenting for your sins from the weekend," she snapped.

Mandy and Maddie's face twisted in awe that someone had dared to challenge them on their behaviour. Her mother didn't give them a chance to respond as she turned on her heel and walked to her. She wrapped her in a hug and they headed home early.

Lexi would like to say that it was the last time her mother held her while she wept over cruel comments. But it wasn't. Her parents never did ask her about the night of the accident and why she had left the party upset. Jack had threatened to beat up everyone until he found out, but at her request stopped. He was so protective and she loved that about him.

A short time later, Mr Hart had arrived for supper and was greeted by all members of the family. Nana only had two children of her own, Jessica and Jackson. Uncle Jackson was available via video chat as he was working out of the country. She and Jack were the only grandchildren and were listed in the will.

Once the meal had been devoured

and the dishes cleared away, the family reconvened in the living room, where her mother sipped on a glass of Chardonnay, while her father held a tumbler of Scotch. Mr Hart was an older man who had been a good friend of Nana's and he was an honest man. He'd been her father's mentor when he was working through law school. The years had been good to Mr Hart, despite his silver hair that sat neatly on his round head and the extra weight around the waist, the man appeared to be ten years younger than his actual age.

Mr Hart sat across from the family in a wingback chair that was placed adjacent to the stone fireplace. He pulled out his briefcase and slipped on his glasses, which always fell down his nose as he read.

"Shall we get started?" he asked.

"Of course, Mr Hart," her mother responded.

"Okay. Mrs Jenkins finalized her will last year after making some final recommendations. I will say that some of the stipulations in the will are ...unconventional," he warned.

"Nothing about Mama was conventional, Mr Hart," Uncle Jackson exclaimed from the iPad being held by her mother. They all chuckled. Nana had her way of doing things and she always wanted to defy what was expected of her.

"Very well. Both of her children have been left trusts in their names, which are each for the amount of two million dollars," he said.

Her mother's eyes widened in surprise. Everyone knew that Nana was from old money, but her lifestyle wasn't lavished or over the top. For God's sake, she ran a horse ranch when she probably didn't have to work at all.

"Are you quite sure, Mr Hart? That is quite a lot of money that we did not know our mother possessed," Uncle Jackson said and her mother nodded her head in agreement.

"I am quite sure. It appears as though your mother had been preparing to ensure your comfort in life upon her departure. Additionally, she left you both letters which are here. Mr Jenkins, if you would like for me to have this directed to your address let me know. I am not permitted to open the letters as they are sealed," he states.

"Sweet baby Jesus," her mother mumbled.

"I am certain that you will find answers in her instructions to both of you. There are no stipulations to these trusts and you will both be provided access to the accounts before I leave tonight," he continued.

"Who would have known that Nana was filthy rich. She worked her own horse ranch for crying out loud," her father exclaimed, reiterating Lexi's thoughts.

"Moving forward is the matter of her farm, which includes all three hundred acres of property, and all building that lay on the property will go to her grandchildren, Lexi and Jack," he announced.

What. The. Fuck.

Jack and Lexi looked at each other with matching expressions of disbelief. The property was worth millions of dollars. Lexi didn't understand why Nana would leave that to them when there were more appropriate options. Lexi and Jack grew up on the ranch, but they knew nothing about running a business.

"You are both listed as co-owners, however, this is where your grandmother's request became unconventional. Your grandmother inserted a clause whereby you both are required to reside on the farm for one year to maintain ownership of the property," Mr Hart said, handing the siblings matching envelopes with their names written across them in their Nana's hand.

"What? Wait, you're saying that for either of us to maintain ownership that we both need to reside on the ranch for a year?" Jack asked. Lexi sat dumbfounded and unable to form words.

"That is correct. Should either you fail to follow the requirements you will both lose out on the property; you cannot sell the property or buy each other out until the year passes. If you fail the property will be placed on the market and the money from this transaction would be donated to a charity of your grandmother's choice," he added.

Lexi sat in the living room, gripping the letter from her Nana in her hand. She never expected her Nana to put her in such a precarious position. Nana knew Lexi was living in New York and had no intention to return to Silverton permanently. Lexi decided to open her letter to see if it helped her gain some clarity on her Nana's intent.

The letter was written in her grandmother's elegant hand and smelt of her unique scent, roses and earl grey tea.

My dearest Lexi,

You're probably wondering about the stipulation I had put in place in my will. I have watched you and Jack grow into amazing and loving people, and I am so proud of both of you for what you've accomplished. But after the accident, you left Silverton never to return for any length of time. You were running because you did not want to stay and face the pain. I know a thing or two about that, Peanut. My greatest wish for you is to not have any regrets when you get where I am. Now is the time for you to face your demons, love. I so wish I could be there to hold your hand as you face this challenge but know that I am there in spirit. I know you like New York, but you never seemed happy there, but you were always so happy at home and on the ranch. I'm just asking that you give it a try, if not for yourself than for Jack. In this envelope is the key to the ranch, as well as any other information you need to know about the business.

I love you to the moon and back, Peanut.

Xo - Nana

"Son of a bitch," Lexi muttered, running her hand down her face.

"Peanut?" her mother's tentative voice pierced her thoughts.

"Mama, I don't know what to do," she confessed.

Things just became way more complicated.

Chapter 7

SAWYER

Sawyer and his family were relieved that Leo was released. Honestly, he didn't think he could manage Jordan if he hadn't been. Leo was forced to work on the ranch after school and would be seeking somewhere to volunteer for his community service. Sawyer hadn't seen Lexi since that day at court, but that was for the best. She certainly did not respond well to their brief encounter before court. He didn't need to give her more reasons to hate him.

On Friday, he made his way to see Sara and Brett as promised. Sara was full of excitement and something in his gut twisted with guilt. He'd been preoccupied lately and hadn't spent as much time with his goddaughter as he should. After they shared a meal, Sara yanked him into her room, where she painted his nails a beautiful shade of pink, topped it off with a tiara and feather boa before they sat down for tea.

"Smile," Brett said from the doorway.

Sawyer looked up and Brett's smile was covered by his phone as he took a photo.

Son of a bitch.

"Oh man, your sister is going to pay good money for these," he chuckled.

Sawyer scowled and eyed Brett. The bastard enjoyed documenting his torment. Lucky for him, Sara was the cutest child to ever walk the earth, so he wouldn't be embarrassed. After his laughter died down, Brett prompted Sara to get ready for bed.

"Will you read me a story, Uncle Sawyer?" she asked.

Who in their right might would deny her anything? All she had to do was push out her little lip and her every desire would be plopped down in front of her.

"You know I never miss a chance to read about Peppa the Pig. She's my girl, ya know?" he said, as he stood and walked out with Brett while Sara got ready for bed.

"I find it hard to believe there is any of you in that sweet innocent child," he said to Brett shaking his head.

"Hey, you haven't seen her have a meltdown in the middle of the grocery store because she couldn't get Lucky Charms," he sighed.

Sawyer shrugged, "That part is all you, my friend."

"I'm ready, Uncle Sawyer!" Sara yelled from her room.

Sawyer left Brett and headed into Sara's room, where she was carefully tucked into her princess bed. She already had several books laid out and had pulled her favourite bunny under the covers with her. She looked exactly like her mother with her bright blue eyes and golden ringlets flanking her face. Lucy had a spirit that brightened every room and a laugh that radiated happiness. He missed her every day, but most of all he missed the way his friend smiled when she was around. It'd been a long time since Brett felt that kind of happiness. And he wanted that for him and Sara.

"Uncle Sawyer," she said, as he sat alongside her bed with her favourite fairy tale book.

"Can you tell me about my mommy?" she asked. Sawyer felt his heart drop at the thought of Sara's life without Lucy. She would have loved to see her grow up, graduate, get married and have a family of her own one day. Brett had always ensured that Sara knew about her mother and let her ask as many questions as she needed.

"Of course, shall I tell you about when you were born?" he asked.

"Oh yes, that's my favourite!" she squealed clapping her little chubby hands together happily.

Sawyer leaned back on her headboard and Sara curled up into his side with her favourite bunny as the star nightlight glowed just enough to see her contented angelic face.

"Well, your mommy and daddy are my best friends. Your daddy and I grew up here together and we got in so much trouble when we were small. Old missus Hart would call us 'double trouble'," her little giggle was muffled as she cuddled closer.

"Your mommy and daddy got married, in this big church with a lot of people. Your daddy wore a fancy suit," he continued.

"Did he look the handsomest?" She asked.

"I'm sure your mommy thought he was, but we all know that I was the most handsome. He looked like a penguin in my opinion," he teased as he stroked her hair gently.

"Your mommy was so beautiful, and before you ask, yes she was by far the most beautiful woman there. They got married and a year later they found out that you were coming into this world. They were overjoyed and your mommy got excited picking out all the pink and princess things for your room. The day you were born was the best day of their lives and mine."

"Yours too?" she asked stifling a yawn and her little eyes began to droop with exhaustion.

"Mine too, because that was the day your mommy and daddy asked me to be your Godfather. And I held you for the very first time and you were so tiny. You were so innocent and beautiful. I knew then, that no matter what, I would help them keep you safe. I would make sure boys ran screaming from the house and embarrass you when I'd see you at the mall with your friends," he whispered.

Her breathing steadied and Sawyer inched his way out from under her hold and kissed her forehead before he closed the door gently. He joined Brett in the kitchen where he was handed a beer and sat across from him at the island.

"So," Brett started, "what are you going to do about Lexi?"

"Why would I do anything about Lexi?" Sawyer asked. Brett rolled his eyes and took another drag on his beer before he answered.

"Because anyone who knows you as well as I do, knows that you loved that girl back in the day. You stayed by her bedside while she recovered, and you're not even sure if she knows that," he challenged.

"Man, she wants nothing to do with me. You could have frozen the creek with the level of cold she tossed my way," he sighed and ran a hand through his chestnut hair.

"I know you've struggled with what went down years ago. I also know that you've changed a lot since then. You're not that stupid little boy anymore, Sawyer. Well, you're not little anymore," he mocked.

"She's only back for a brief time, Brett. It won't do either of us any good by rehashing the past," he offered.

"Word around town is that she'll be staying a bit longer than expected," he cooed.

Sawyer stopped drinking for a moment before he laid his bottle down. He couldn't process what his friend said to him. Lexi had visited several times over the years, but she always returned to New York. Sure, he'd made attempts over the years to engage her, but she always brushed him off.

"Why would she?" he asked Brett.

Sawyer was genuinely confused as to why Brett would make such a comment. He knew everything there was to know about the night of Lexi's accident. Meaning, he knew how Sawyer felt about her and how just hearing her name had a drastic impact on him.

"According to Jack, her Nana left them both the ranch and they have to live on it for a year or lose it all. Jack said his sister is still trying to figure out a loophole but there's none that they know of," he smiled.

"Wait, you mean the ranch Mrs Jenkins owned next to McGuire's ranch?" he asked, his shock unable to be wiped off his face.

"That very one," Brett said with a smug look on his stupid face.

One baseball game and plate of nachos later and Sawyer headed home to the ranch to find comfort in his king-sized bed when a call from dispatch caught his ear. It was reported that there was a minor accident on Route 86 between a white BMW and a Ford F 150. Sawyer recognized the BMW to be Lexi's since she was the only one in their small town with such a fancy piece of crap besides Jordan. Jordan's car was bright red, so he ruled her out.

The Deputy on duty was handling a domestic call and the accident would have to wait until he was finished. Sawyer wished at that moment that they had more resources to better serve the town. He wasn't willing to let Lexi sit on the side of the road while he passed by, so he picked up his radio and advised Cindy, the dispatcher, that he would take the call as he was in the area.

Sawyer rolled up on the scene, where the F 150 had rear-ended Lexi's BMW. There was a large built man crotched by the driver side door of Lexi's car. He jumped out of his car and approached. He heard sobs and a gruff voice attempting to soothe.

"Is everyone okay?" he asked moving closer. The damage was minor but the stricken expression on the man told him that something was not right. The man stood and moved back from the car, where a distraught Lexi held her head in her hands and rocked back and forth as she sobbed.

He shifted closer and bent down placing a hand on her shoulder. He hoped the contact wouldn't cause her to become escalated.

"Lexi, sweetheart, are you hurt?" he asked softly.

Lexi rocked and was counting from what he heard of her mumbled words. He took his time to assess whether she had any injuries, but there was no blood or any obvious signs of injury.

"1...2...3...4...5...6..." she mumbled trying to catch her breath in between sobs.

Sawyer reached over and unlocked the seat belt and placed another hand on her shoulder as he tried to get her attention.

"Lex, it's me, Sawyer. Can you look at me, darling?" he asked. At his name, her head popped up and he caught sight of the tears flooding her eyes and long black streaks from mascara covered her cheeks. She turned her head and her eyes met him, but hers were glassed as though she wasn't present in the here and now.

"Sawyer?" she asked. "No, not Sawyer, anyone but Sawyer," she blurted before she crumpled over wheezing.

Sawyer's heart broke into a million pieces at the thought that she wanted anyone but him to help her. He'd sat with her through the night terrors when she was in the hospital and she may not remember that, but he did. As gently as possible, he lifted her from the car and she clung to him as though he was the answer to the world's unknown mysteries. She was so small and he thought that if he squeezed hard enough, he would break her. He heard the sirens of the ambulance headed their way, but the sirens caused Lexi to flinched and he knew the sound triggered her memories. He quickly radioed and asked the paramedics to not play the siren.

He held Lexi in his arms as he leaned against the side of her car. He rubbed her back and cradled her protectively against his chest. She began to calm and her breathes came slow and steady. She looked up at him and the pain he saw in her eyes was his undoing. This strong, fierce and smart-mouthed woman was falling to pieces in his arms.

"Sawyer?" she asked, her voice low and vulnerable.

"Yes, Sugar, I'm here," he whispered.

"Oh God," she huffed jumping back from his arms. She stumbled and he reached out to steady her, but she flinched out of his reach.

"Don't touch me," she gritted out. Sawyer put up his hands and backed away to reassure her that he wouldn't.

"Lexi, I got here and you were hysterical. I had to get you out of the car to see if you were injured," he said.

"I'm fine," she muttered wiping the mascara from her cheeks frantically.

"I'm sure you are, but let the paramedics take a look at you," Sawyer said, as the paramedics approached.

"No, I'm fine. Just a little shook up," she turned towards the paramedics, "I'm okay, I don't need any medical help, thank you," she said.

She straightened herself and Sawyer saw the facade of the ice queen switch on her face. She walked toward the man and assessed the damage to her car. They exchanged contact information, and Lexi strutted toward him.

"Thank you for responding, Sheriff, but there is no damage and neither of us wish to make a formal complaint," she said coldly.

She had to be crazy if she thought that he was going to let her panic attack slide under the radar. She had once been the girl he loved and he wouldn't let her go until he was sure she would be okay. The paramedics and the man in the Ford drove off, which left Lexi and Sawyer standing in the intersection in an odd stare down.

"I'm not letting you go until I know you're okay," he said.

"I'm fine, you have done your duty, Sheriff, I am no longer in need of your assistance," she sneered but was unable to meet his eye. She made to turn away from him, so he caught her elbow and turned her to face him.

"Lexi, I'm here as a friend," he said unable to force his stare away from her face.

"We stopped being friends a long

time ago, Sawyer," she argued.

He raised his hand and swiped his knuckles over her cheek, causing her eyes to close at his touch. He studied the dark circles under her beautiful hazel eyes and felt the warmth silkiness of her skin.

"Maybe you did, Lex. But I never stopped caring about you, ever," he whispered, as his eyes glanced to her lips. His hand cupped her chin as she licked her bottom lip and he tilted his head closer to her face. Her soft delicate lips were a breath away from his and he desperately wanted to taste her. But she moved back and out of his grasp.

"That's not what I remember, Sawyer," she said, as she got in her car and drove away. Sawyer was left standing in the road wondering how he could persuade Lexi to speak with him. He needed to clear the air if it was the last thing he did.

Chapter 8

LEXI

Lexi was still reeling from the encounter with Sawyer Friday night when her boss called from New York to discuss her request for a leave of absence. Since the shock of Nana's will had settled, she realized that she needed to stay and help her brother. Jack dreamt of owning his own ranch and she wouldn't stand in the way of that.

Mr Harper was the District Attorney and he was the typical boys club member who thought women belonged in the kitchen and not in the courtroom. She worked hard to prove to the partners that she was a strong lawyer, but she feared that asking for the leave would cast her in a different light.

"Mr Harper, Thank you for returning my call," she said from the window seat in her bedroom.

"Ms Scott, I understand you have encountered some family issues and have requested a leave of absence from your position, is that correct?" he asked, his displeasure spilt through the phone.

"Yes, I am sorry to have to request, but I am legally required to remain in Silverton until conditions of the will are met," she added.

He coughed loudly, "Well, we are unable to hold your position at the firm for any longer than six months. We have many valuable cases that depend on reliable staff but you're a damn good prosecutor and I don't want to lose you. How about you take six months and see if you can find some way to return to New York. If there isn't a resolution, we will have to consider alternatives," he sighed.

Her shoulders dropped and the strain in her neck radiated to her head, a sure sign that there was a migraine in her future.

"I understand Mr Harper. Thank you for considering the request," she added.

She hung up the phone and made her way downstairs where her brother was supposed to meet her so they could visit the ranch. Sure enough, he was in the kitchen devouring some of Mama's leftover peach cobbler. She leaned against the doorway as she watched her brother empty the contents of the refrigerator.

"What are you going to do when we move out to the ranch and mama isn't around to cook for you?" she teased.

Jack shrugged, "She'll make sure I'm fed."

Lexi rolled her eyes and made her way into the kitchen and sat across from her brother. Maybe the experience would be good for them. They'd been apart for so long, it almost felt as though she didn't know who he was anymore. Could that be what her Nana meant about being happy? Jack interrupted her moment of thought by trying to speak with his mouth full.

"So, does that mean you're going to stay?" he asked.

She sighed, "Yes, my boss gave me six months and if I can't return after then

I suspect I'll lose my position." She ran her hand through her hair, a nervous habit she couldn't shake.

Jack rounded the island and grabbed Lexi in a bear hug. He'd been worried about whether she would agree to the terms in the will. He said that he would be okay either way, but they both knew that the ranch was part of their family and neither wanted to see it sold off.

"You're the best sister, ever," he exclaimed, as Lexi dangled limply from his embrace. There was no point in fighting it, that was something she learnt a long time ago.

"Munchkin, I'm your only sister," she replied.

He set her down and made his way to the front door, "And thank the Lord for that. I don't think this world could handle another Lexi Scott."

Lexi walked behind him as they jumped in his truck and made their way out to Jenkin's Ranch. The drive to the ranch had always been one of Lexi's favourites. The dirt road tossed back dirt that mirrored clouds, and tractors were seen cutting hay. In the fall, pumpkins grew at the Benson Ranch, and families could be seen picking out the perfect one with their children. Wild stallions often raced through the pastures where cows and sheep grazed under the hot sun of Texas. The scent of manure and grass permeated the air. The smell she'd associated with home.

The Jenkin's Ranch was three hundred acres that included several pastures, bunkhouses, cabins, and the main house. In the summer season, Nana always rented the cabins out to folks looking to experience the ranching life. Lexi and Jack did their part in helping during the busy times and would even take the folks on hayrides and horseback riding. They'd spent their summers with Nana and only went home to sleep.

They pulled off the main road and up the drive to the ranch. The big red mailbox stood sentinel at the beginning of the drive. Nana always loved that ugly old thing. If Lexi had a nickel for every time a bunch of boys knocked it off with a bat, she could afford the whole God damn farm. Nana knew it was ugly but kept it just to piss Papa off. The ugly old mailbox was the exact opposite of the farmhouse that came into view minutes later.

Overlooking a dazzling lake, the three thousand square foot country home encompassed the nucleus of the ranch. The fire truck red of the house stood out on the green backdrop. There was a wrap-around porch that encircles the whole outside of the house, with a wooden porch swing that was made by their grandfather. It was the place where she received her first kiss at the age of thirteen.

They stopped in front of the house and jumped out before walking to the steps. Lexi paused a moment and felt herself becoming emotional. So many memories were wrapped up in the walls of that house and that house held secrets, she was sure of that. But now, it was to be their home and it was their turn to make their family proud.

"You ready, sis?" Jack asked placing a hand on her shoulders.

Lexi fought back the sting of tears

that surfaced and nodded before they walked together up the steps and into their Nana's home. Lexi could still smell her perfume and hear her laughter as she entered the house. Jack must've sensed her emotions because he gripped her hand and intertwined their fingers as they strode through the house.

"Mom and dad have kept the place going since Nana passed, so the place doesn't even look different than we last saw it," Jack said.

"It doesn't look different, but it is," she retorted.

They took the stairs to the second floor, but neither of them made the move to enter Nana's room. They weren't ready to handle that just yet, but they would at some point over the next twelve months. After they'd done a walkthrough of the home, Lexi sat on the front porch swing while Jack spoke with the ranch hands about the schedule and routine. He was made for running a ranch and she saw the joy he had for the work. She wouldn't leave him and risk him losing it because of her dreams. He deserved to have some happiness in his life and as his big sister, she'd do everything in her power to make sure he got it.

"I think we should ride the fence line to get a better idea of what we got going here," Jack called from the front yard.

"I'd like that. It's been a long time since I rode a horse though," she stood and made her way toward the barn with her brother in tow.

"Well, I'm sure there's a pretty mare in here that you'll find to your liking," he smiled as they entered the barn.

Lexi gasped when she saw the mare Jack had the ranch hand saddle for her. Her name was Beauty and she was an amazing all black stallion. Her mother was bred at the ranch and was the mare she learnt how to ride on. Once her mother had passed away, Beauty became her regular riding horse and like everything else, she left her behind ten years ago.

"Oh, Jack! She's still here," Lexi wasn't able to stop the tears that flowed down her cheeks at the sight of Beauty. The mare seemed to recognize her and immediately nuzzled her neck as she rubbed her mane.

"Nana couldn't part with her after you left. She said she knew you'd be back to claim her one day," he said as came up behind her and kissed her on top of the head.

"Now, let's go ride the line, sis," he ordered.

Lexi wasted no time hoisting herself onto the back of Beauty and after a couple of minutes of riding, she felt as though she never left. Their fence line happened to back onto several other ranches, one of which was the McGuire family farm. They were an operating cattle farm, whereas the Jenkin's Farm bred horses.

As they continued along the fence line, they spotted several riders in the distance. She felt a slight tingle on the back of her neck and didn't have to look to know it was Sawyer. She hadn't told anyone about her panic attacks since the accident beside her doctor. Sawyer had been there during one of her episodes and she didn't know if she could face him. That aside, there was the small issue of the almost kiss and what he said about caring about her.

He rode up to them on a chocolate stallion, with his black cowboy hat, ripped jeans and a five o'clock shadow that she longed to rub against. The man oozed sex and she hated it. Or she tried damn hard to hate it.

"Howdy Jack!" Sawyer greeted.

"How's it going, Sheriff?" Jack replied.

"Since we're neighbours now, Sawyer will do just fine," Sawyer said, taking off his cowboy hat and using the back of his hand to wipe sweat from his brow.

Jack sensed tension between the two and decided he wanted none of it. So like all baby brothers, he made a lame excuse to leave.

"If you'll excuse me, Sawyer, I'm just running the line. Lex, I'll meet you in the middle?" he asked, his brow raised to question if she was okay.

She nodded her agreement and watched as her jackass brother left her to fend for herself with the hot as hell new neighbour. Without a word said, she turned Beauty and trotted the opposite way of the fence, but Sawyer wasn't deterred and followed her on his side.

"How you feeling after the other night?" he asked, not beating around the bush, he just came out and asked taking her by surprise.

"I'm fine," she mumbled.

"Lexi, does that happen often when you drive?"

She didn't want to have that conversation with anyone, let alone the man who broke her heart and sent her running to New York. But she also knew that Sawyer would continue to ask questions until he got an answer.

"It's happened a couple of times since the accident, but it's been a while since an attack has come on," she said honestly. She kept her eyes forward as she feared if she looked at him she would see pity etched across his face, and the last thing she wanted was pity.

"Lexi," he started, and she already knew the tone and the follow-up speech that was coming, so she shut it down.

"Sawyer, I don't need your pity. I've moved on with my life just fine since the accident. I may never wow people with my beauty but I really couldn't care less about it," she argued.

"Hey now, don't say that. You're beautiful and any asshole who doesn't see that is an idiot," he added. She looked over at him and saw no pity in his eyes, just sadness.

"You don't need to spare my feelings, Sawyer. It's not like you had any problems saying it like it was before," she snapped.

He pulled his horse to a stop and asked, "What's that supposed to mean?"

Did he not remember why she left the party that night? Maybe it was time to enlighten the famed playboy of the McGuire men.

"You don't remember do you?" she asked, as she moved Beauty closer to the fence so she could face him.

"We were young Lexi. I was stupid and a genuine jackass, but I'd hoped after all this time that we could move forward. I thought we had a good time before I was a jackass, and it's a special memory for me," he hesitated.

She was pissed now. He was lying to himself and her if he said that their intimate encounter was special to him. She jumped off her horse and made it to the fence. He did the same.

"That night, when we, you know," she said.

"Had sex," Sawyer smirked.

"Yes, that. Well, that was my first time," she muttered.

Sawyer's jaw dropped to the ground and a fierce blush rose in her cheeks. She was sure her   face was on fire from the embarrassment.

"Jesus, I had no idea! How come you didn't tell me? Lexi, you deserved more for your first time," he expressed.

Lexi rolled her eyes. She was nothing if not practical. She never expected roses and candlelight to commemorate the night she lost her innocence. It wasn't about where or how it was about who she shared it with. She raised her hand to stop his tangent.

"Stop. It was never about what I deserved, Sawyer. We were friends and that night I felt as though we were more than that. You had always been the one I wanted to share that with, but I never got the feeling you felt the same," she continued.

"Lexi," he attempted to interrupt, but she refused.

"No, I need you to listen to me. I've bottled so much hatred and hurt about that night. About how we finally came together and how everything was ripped apart,"

"The accident…" he murmured.

"My heart broke long before the accident, Sawyer. It broke when after I had sex for the first time with the guy of my dreams only to hear him say that I was nothing to him. That's what caused me to leave the party early and to be crying as I ran. It was the last thing I remembered before I hit the pavement after that drunk driver hit me," she choked out.

"Lexi, please let me explain," he begged.

She stepped back and shook her

head, "There is nothing you can say that will change it, Sawyer!"

"I may have received some ugly scars from the accident, but the scar that hurts the most is here," she pointed to her heart, "You took part of it that night and I never learned to use it again. For that, I can never forgive you."

With that said, she hopped on Beauty and rode away from the boy who broke her heart and the man who could break what was left of it.

Chapter 9

SAWYER

Sawyer stood shocked as he watched Lexi ride off. That hadn't been how he thought that conversation would go. He felt like a complete dick and wanted to go back in time to punch eighteen-year-old Sawyer in the junk.

It was her first time.

He was going to hell.

If he had known he never would have hooked up with her. He had no idea what he was thinking back then, but he knew that the man he was now, was not okay leaving things like that with Lexi. He needed to make it up to her and show her that he wasn't that boy anymore.

He leaned over the fence, as Remi approached riding that huge beast he called

Shadow. Remi was a Texas man and lived by the "go big or go home" motto. Everything was bigger, his house, truck, his horse and of course his belt buckle.

"You look like someone killed your puppy. What's wrong?" Remi asked, as his Texas drawl spewed like honey from his lips.

Damn Remi and his luck. The dickhead found the love of his life, married her and has never been happier.   Meanwhile, Sawyer still prowled the bar on the weekends and never stayed the night with a woman out of fear they would get the wrong idea.

"I fucked up, Rem," he groaned.

"You're gonna have to be more specific…" he replied.

There was nothing worse than having to admit to your older brother that you were a dickhead who disrespected a good woman. There were many things Remi couldn't stand, and a man disrespecting a woman was one of them.

He mounted his horse and on the ride back to their ranch, he unleashed the full story on Remi. He stayed silent for a long time afterwards and Sawyer didn't know if that was a good thing or a bad thing. They settled the horses and made their way into the main house to wash up.

"So, what are ya going to do?" he asked Sawyer.

"That's kind of why I thought to talk to you Rem. I'm way out of my wheelhouse here. I have no idea how to make it up to Lexi and show her that I'm not like that. I was a dumb kid trying to fit in and be cool," Sawyer admitted.

Remi made his way to the kitchen, where he pecked Aubrey on the lips before stealing two beers from the fridge. They were on their way to the porch when a truck pulled up in the drive. Neither of them had seen the truck before and were immediately suspicious until the driver stepped out.

"Son of a bitch," Remi hollered, before jumping down the steps and running to the visitor. Sawyer trailed behind him eager to get to their guest.

"Finn, how come you never told us

you were in?" Sawyer asked as he embraced his brother in a manly hug.

Finn had been deployed for a year overseas and it marked his fourth deployment. He'd occasionally returned to American soil, but normally he'd call to let everyone know to expect him. Every time he saw his brother, he noted differences. He always returned bigger than before. Sawyer often joked about him needing to get specialty made shirts to accommodate his biceps. He had the typical McGuire green eyes; his skin had bronzed and his hair was buzzed short. He carried himself differently this time, and Sawyer knew that his brother had been through something significant since the last time he was home.

Sawyer's return to civilian life was a challenge when he was discharged at twenty-four. His time in the Navy SEALs left a mark on his spirit that could never be removed. His SEAL brothers still kept in touch, some were still deployed, some didn't make it back, all came back with scars.

"I needed a couple of days to get my

head on straight before I came back here. Plus, I missed a wedding and needed to impress my new sister in law," Finn smiled, as he and Remi climbed the stairs to the main house.

"Miss Martha, we managed to pick up a stray on our adventures today," Remi yelled.

"A stray? Boy... you best be talking about a cat," she scolded, as she rounded the corner from the kitchen. The moment her eyes landed on Finn; her eyes filled with tears. Miss Martha never had children of her own, but the McGuires had become her family and she felt their pain the same as any mother would.

Miss Martha stayed rooted in place as her hand rose to her lips and tears fell down her cheeks. Finn moved toward her.

"Hey Miss Martha, I hope you don't mind me dropping in without calling first," Finn said. Miss Martha embraced him in her arms in a loving hug that all the McGuires had felt at one point or another in their lives.

"Welcome home, my boy. This is

where you belong, you don't need to call ahead. I'm just happy you're back," she wiped the tears from her face and took in Finn. "And what the heck have they been feeding you? I'm gonna need to live in the grocery store to keep you boys going in food," she laughed.

"Hey! What's all the commotion about?" Aubrey stepped into the house and immediately went to Remi's side. He placed a chaste kiss on her temple before he made introductions.

"Finn, this is Aubrey. My wife," Remi announced, gleaming with pride when he called her his wife.

Finn turned and looked at Aubrey wrapped in the arms of Remi, completely contented to live there forever. The smile on Remi's face seemed to grow every time they were together. It was sickening.

"So, this is the new sister," he asked, in his serious Army Ranger voice. Then he moved toward Aubrey and picked her up in his arms in a strong bear hug. Aubrey yelped in surprise but slowly began to laugh. He twirled her a couple of times before returning her to Remi.

"I'm looking forward to getting to know you, Finn. At least while you're here," Aubrey said.

"About that," Finn started, "I'm not returning to the Rangers or the Army. So I'll be around indefinitely if that's okay with everyone else?" he announced.

Silence fell over the house as everyone took in the news that Finn shared. Sawyer knew the challenges he would face reintegrating into civilian society, and he would be there for his brother as he battled those demons.

"Your room is exactly the way you left it," Miss Martha cheered.

"This is home, Finn. Welcome home," Aubrey continued.

The rest of the evening passed without incident as Finn talked about his time overseas, or what he could tell them. Jordan and Daisy arrived shortly after Finn arrived. Both were ecstatic that Finn would be staying home and Jordan had already enlisted his help with Leo. After supper, when the dishes were put away and the night started to whine down, the siblings gathered on the front porch in their designated chairs.

He listened as his family talked about their lives and something inside him felt as though he was missing something. As he looked at Aubrey snuggled onto Remi's lap, he realized what he was missing. Love. That didn't mean that there wasn't love in his life, there was, but the love of a woman, a future of possibility and family. Lexi popped into his head and he wondered why she would. With the excitement of Finn's return, he hadn't the chance to continue the conversation with Remi about what he should do.

He knew he had to start somewhere, so he figured he needed to do some serious wooing just to get her to give him the time of day. He tossed and turned that night as the uneasy feeling settled on his chest. For whatever reason, Lexi's opinion of him mattered and the fact that she was hurt by him mattered. He couldn't leave it and not at least try to make it up to her.

The next morning, he took a detour on his way to the office. He stopped into the local florist and had a dozen blush pink roses sent to Lexi at her parent's home. He didn't know if she'd moved to the ranch yet, so to be safe, her parents 'place was the best alternative.

On the card he wrote:

Let me make it up to you.

Love: SMG

He entered his office with the thoughts that it would be a great day. He had a plan on how to get Lexi to talk to him and his brother had returned from war in one piece. He was walking on sunshine until he opened his office door and came toe to toe with a large man in a black suit. Sawyer's gaze ran up over the man before he shifted and moved toward his desk.

"Can I help you?" he asked, a bit peeved that the suit was in his office in the first place.

"I'm Agent Phillips from the FBI. I have some information I thought would be good to share with local police," he said robotically.

"Okay, have a seat and tell me about this information," Sawyer instructed.

"Raymond Brant is a serial killer who

was incarcerated in a federal facility in New York State. He was convicted of murdering twelve different women and dumping their bodies in Central Park with a note stapled to their chests," Phillips laid a file folder on his desk, "We have information to believe that he could be coming to this area."

"I thought you said he was incarcerated?" he questioned, glancing through the gruesome file in his hands.

"He was incarcerated, but during transport to court, he found a way to disarm the guard and escape. We believe he'd pose a risk to anyone involved in the case," he said sharply.

"I still don't understand what this has to do with Silverton," he challenged.

Phillips sighed, "I have reason to believe that the lead prosecutor is staying here, Lexi Scott."

Sawyer's attention peaked at the mention of Lexi's name. His head tipped up from the file he was scanning. A cold shiver ran through him at the thought that Lexi was connected to any of the scum she put away back in New York.

"Ms Scott is staying here with her parents, but she also has a ranch near mine. Are you trying to say that Lexi could be a target for Brant?" his heart pounded in his chest at the thought of Lexi on Brant's radar.

Phillips moved forward to place his elbows on his thighs. "Sheriff, Ms Scott is responsible for incarcerating Brant and sentencing him to twelve life sentences. The man would never see the light of day again. During the trial, Ms Scott received threats from him regularly and we assigned an agent to her for her safety. Now that Brant has escaped custody, I believe Ms. Scott will be his number one target," he claimed.

Sawyer pulled his hand down his face. He didn't like the idea of Lexi being unguarded while she was in Texas. If Brant tried to get to her and hurt her, he'd never be able to live with himself.

"I'll have a guard assigned to her while she is in Texas. Should she return to New York this office will contact you. Does Lexi know what's happening? Have you spoken to her?" he asked.

"No and honestly, Sheriff, I'm not here in an official capacity," he admitted. "But my conscious would not settle until I knew Ms. Scott was aware of the threat."

Sawyer stood and offered his hand to Phillips, "Thank you, I'll be sure to have someone follow up with her and have this photo circulated," he confirmed.

He escorted Agent Phillips and stopped by Parker's desk to hand him the photo. Brant didn't stand out and would be hard to find unless his deputies knew what they were looking for. A white middle-aged man, with brown hair, brown eyes and in his mid-forties, would blend into Silverton without any issues.

"Parker, can you please circulate this to the others. Tell them if they spot this man to call me directly and to apprehend him," Sawyer instructed, as he grabbed his cowboy hat and keys.

Parker looked up from the photo, "Where you headed to, Sheriff?" he asked.

"I have to go see Ms Scott. You can reach me by phone," Sawyer said.

He left the office and drove directly

to Jenkin's ranch, where he suspected Lexi would be with her brother. He wouldn't let anyone get near Lexi and he made it his mission to ensure she stayed safe while in Silverton.

Chapter 10

LEXI

Lexi spent her day shopping with her mother on Main Street. It was the only way to get her to stop asking about the flowers she'd received that morning. Luckily Sawyer didn't sign his name and left initials.

Regardless, her mother was on round three hundred and forty-six of guess and Lexi manipulated her into shopping. Her mother loved doing "girly" things with her when she visited. Her mother also knew everyone in the small county and they were stopped every couple of minutes when someone spotted her. She was browsing through dresses in a boutique when someone walked by the glass and she immediatcly recognized him.

Finn.

Finn McGuire was one of her favourite people when they were growing up. She knew from her mother that he enlisted in the Army when he graduated from High School. He was a year or two younger than her and Sawyer, but he was so charismatic that he made friends instantly with anyone he met.

"Hey Mama, I just spotted an old friend, I'm just going to pop outside for a second," she said through the dressing room door to her mother. Lexi didn't give her time to answer before she was out of the store. She saw Finn place an order at the local coffee spot and made her way to him. She also needed another fix of caffeine if she was going to keep up with her mother's shopping spree.

Finn looked different, but she expected that. War took its toll on those who served. He'd beefed up since the last time she saw him, but his smile was still the same as it had always been — charming and intoxicating.

She stood behind Finn in the line for coffee but wasted no time moving in front of him to say hello. She had forgotten how much bigger he was than her. At six foot three, he towered over her five foot six, even in her highest heels she wouldn't even come to his nose.

"Hey Finn," she greeted.

He eyed her speculatively before he realized who she was. Lexi saw when realization dawned on him.

"Lexi Scott!" he said gleefully.

Before she knew what was happening she was lifted off her feet and taken into the best bear hug she'd ever had. Finn spent a lot of time on the Ranch when they were growing up. Although Lexi was older, he had a great friendship with Jack. Once Finn released her from his grip, they placed their orders and Finn invited her to sit and catch up.

The coffee spot was small, but they made the best coffee in the county. The owner had Nora Jones blasting through the overhead speakers, and there were tables, couches and bean bag chairs around the place. It was a hipster's paradise.

"When did you get back?" Lexi

asked.

"A couple of weeks ago, but I stayed in California for a couple of weeks to clear my head before I came down here to deal with my rowdy siblings," he answered.

Lexi chuckled. She knew a thing or two about the McGuire clan and growing up she was envious of them. They all fit together so well and looked like the perfect family from the outside.

"How long will you be back before you head out again?" Lexi posed.

The mention of another deployment caused Finn's face to fall. He had already been through four tours and had moved up in the Army. As much as she knew that Finn loved serving his country, she also knew that it wasn't something he could do forever. Every time he returned home, his PTSD caused him issues, and he struggled to integrate back into civilian life.

"I think this last one was it for me," he confessed.

"You're ready for that?" she asked, reaching across the table to touch the top of his hand. She knew Finn struggled with that decision. He'd seen the most horrendous and evil acts in the world during his time with the Army. He grabbed her hand and interlocked their fingers.

"Yeah, I am," he nodded. "I always knew that there would come a time when it would no longer fulfil what I need. I want to settle down, have a family, get a regular job. But it's not fair for me to make my wife and children wonder if I'm going to make it back this time or that time."

"Well, you know if you ever want to talk about things, I'm around. Looks like I'm going to be around for at least 12 months," she sighed.

"Why 12 months?" Finn asked, his head popped up from his stare at his coffee lid.

"Nana put a clause in her will that for me and Jack to keep the ranch we both needed to stay there for a year."

Finn's mouth dropped open as he processed what she had told him.

"What about New York? You have a great job there and you're a damn good prosecutor,"

She shook her head and dropped her gaze to her coffee cup lid. She knew she wouldn't find any loopholes in her Nana's will and that she'd stay in Silverton. She knew she would lose everything she worked for in New York, but she couldn't take the ranch away from Jack. She wouldn't be able to live with herself if she did.

Lexi's phone rang, interrupting their conversation. She glanced at the caller ID and noticed it was her father.

"It's my dad, I'm just going to take this," she said.

Finn rose from his seat, pressed a chaste kiss to her cheek.

"It was nice seeing you, Lex. We should catch up again sometime," he winked as he walked out of the shop. She turned to her phone and pressed the answer button.

"Hey, daddy,"

"Peanut, where are you?" his voice was tense and serious, which caused her radar to snap to attention. Her father rarely let things bother him, so she knew that whatever was going on was serious.

"I'm at the coffee shop. Daddy what's wrong?"

"Peanut, the Sheriff is at the Ranch with Jack. He said he needed to talk to you about an urgent matter and would prefer to do that in person," he replied.

Did that man honestly think that he could dictate when she met with him and how? She prided herself on maintaining her patience, but Sawyer was pushing every button and she was ready to flip her bitch switch on his ass.

"Well, you can let the Sheriff know that I will be there once me and Mama are done shopping," she said before she hung up the phone.

Who did Sawyer McGuire thing he was, telling her to drop everything and go meet him? All the other ladies in the county may drop everything — including their knickers — to be his afternoon de-light, but she wouldn't. It would be a cold day in hell before she jumped whenever Sawyer McGuire needed an audience with her.

With that decided, Lexi took her latte and walked the short distance to the boutique where her mother was spending way too much money. As she walked slowly through the street, she took in the sun on her face and the warmth of the rays. She smelt the gardenias and sweet peas in the warm breeze. Storefronts had the beautiful flowers accentuating their shops, which added a vibrant splash of colour to the otherwise bare street. The cobblestone street-hardened her footsteps and combined with the array of colour and iron streetlamps, Lexi felt as though she had taken a step into a different time.

Lexi felt a slight chill spread through her body. She felt as though there were eyes on her from somewhere, so she took the time to search around. She didn't spot anything out of order, but the hair on her arms stood at attention. She dismissed her feelings as irrational and tried to push them out of her head. She'd had her share of threats from clients when she was in New York, but surely no one would think to follow her to Silverton. A new person in that small of a place would stand out, she thought. She was engulfed in her thoughts when someone bellowed behind her.

"Lexi!" her mother hollered, as she strolled down the sidewalk toward her with an immense number of bags hanging from each of her arms.

"Mama, you scared the shit out of me," she admitted.

"Oh darling, I'm sorry! But please, good southern ladies don't use words such as shit," she fell into step with her daughter.

She loved goading her mother when she talked about southern mannerisms. Lexi was taught that good southern ladies kept their mouths and legs closed and their appearances appeasing. Lexi always challenged her mother and kicked up a ruckus when her mother insisted that she go through cotillion. She hated every moment of the experience. She preferred to be mucking stalls and riding horse over pretty dresses and table manners.

"But Mama, what does a southern lady say when she thinks something is bull-shit?" she asked.

Her mother gasped but saw the teasing expression on Lexi's face. She swatted her daughter's arm jokingly, making Lexi laugh. She was so easy to pick on. It was unbelievable to think that she lived happily with her father and two children who found it fun to pick on her.

Mama's phone rang as they approached the car that was parked along the side of the street. Lexi had taken her car and she often forced herself to drive since the accident. Her mother never questioned her insistence on driving and she never explained.

Her mother answered her phone and stood on the sidewalk while Lexi walked around the hood of the car to the driver's side. She had to wait briefly for a car to pass before she made for her door. Her mother was still on the phone and Lexi waited for her to finish. The traffic wasn't busy so she leaned back from her car. She was digging in her purse for her keys when a car started down the road at full speed. Lexi didn't hear the car approach and didn't realize she was dangerously close until her mother screamed.

"Lexi!"

Lexi turned in time to register what was about to happen if she didn't act. In a split second, she jumped onto the hood of her car and rolled to the ground. Her purse was not as fortunate and was ran over by the car. Lexi hit the ground hard and felt a warm trickle above her left eyebrow. She turned over and touched her face. When she looked at her hands they were covered in blood.

The next thing she knew, she was back to the night of the accident ten years ago. Tears streamed down her face as she stepped off the curb in her strappy heels. She felt the impact of the car and heard the smash of glass as she collided with the windshield. She heard the screaming of sirens and the yelling of the bystanders who came to help. Her left temple throbbed and her vision blurred. A voice knocked her out of the trance. It was her mother. She was yelling and holding onto Lexi's shoulders as she collapsed on the sidewalk.

"Lexi! Lexi! Speak to be God damn

it!" her mother bellowed, as she shook Lexi's shoulders. Lexi chuckled before she spoke to her mother.

"I don't think a good southern woman cusses, Mama," she laughed, but it deflated when she felt the tears sting her face and saw the blood on her hands.

"Your father is on his way for us. We need to get you to a hospital," she shrieked.

Lexi moved to stand up and staggered briefly before righting herself. Her vision was fine, but she conceded that she shouldn't be driving right now. Next thing she heard was sirens and the flash of annoying lights as a patrol car pulled aside her car. Out came a man more annoying than the damn lights. Why did he always show up when she was at her weakest?

"I'm fine Sawyer!" she shouted, as he prowled toward her.

"You're not fine, Lexi. You're bleeding for Christ's sake!" he said before he put his hand to her face. She hissed as he touched her cut and she swatted his man hands from her face.

"I have a first aid kit. Stay here," he

ordered.

"Aye aye, Captain!" she said sarcastically, giving him a clumsy salute. Her mother was next to her talking to her father on the phone.

"Did you catch the person in the car?" Sawyer asked when he returned with the first aid kit, laid it on the hood of her car, and dug out some wipes.

"No, I'm sure it was my fault. I should have been more cautious," she admitted.

He used an antiseptic wipe to clean up her wound. His touch was gentle, which was unexpected given the size of his man hands. He looked in her eyes as she winced when the alcohol touched her cut.

"So, am I going to live?" she asked.

He grinned, "You won't need stitches, but we need to talk Lexi."

"No offence Sheriff, but we don't do talking very well," she countered, as he applied a bandage to the cut on her head.

"We didn't always have such a hard time talking, Lex," he said, putting away the first aid kit. Lexi heard the sadness in his voice when he said that.

"What the heck is going on?" Finn announced himself from the sidewalk. He immediately walked towards Lexi with a concerned look shadowing his face.

"It's nothing Finn," she assured.

"It is something Lex. You're bleeding for Christ's sake," he challenged. For the love of God, did the McGuires share the same brain?

"It was just a minor incident, but the Sheriff here, has been very attentive," she said.

Finn wasted no time pulling Lexi into a hug. She and Finn had always been close, but what she didn't realize was how much she missed his friendship. Sawyer stood back and observed the interaction. She almost thought that he was jealous, at least the vein that pulsed on his forehead said he was bothered.

"You okay to drive?" Finn asked, bringing his hands to cup the sides of her face.

"I'm going to give her a ride. We need to talk anyway," Sawyer interrupted.

Finn nodded and turned to Lexi's

mother, who'd finished speaking with her father. Finn was always a gentleman, so it was no surprise when he offered to give Lexi's mother a ride home. Jessica declined but kissed him on the cheek to thank him before she asked Lexi for her keys.

"I'll see you around Lex," he leaned down and pressed a kiss to her forehead. "Sawyer, I'll see ya later?" he questioned.

Sawyer nodded and turned back to Lexi. As Finn walked away her mother leaned in to hug her before she left in Lexi's car.

"You sure you're going to be okay, Peanut?"

"Yes Ma, I'll be just fine," she smiled, hoping it was reassuring.

As her mother pulled back and made her way to the driver's side door, she turned to Lexi.

"I always liked that boy," she nodded her head in the direction Finn had gone. "Maybe you should consider exploring whether there is more than friendship there. You aren't getting any younger sweetie, and I'd like some grandbabies to fuss over," she teased. "Oh! Is he the one who sent the lovely flowers this morning?"

"No..." Lexi said flatly.

Jessica shook her head, "Its a shame you gave them to old Miss Harrington. Maybe you should be open to the possibilities, dear. I want some grandbabies to spoil."

Lexi scoffed, "Trust me, Ma, I don't think Jack will have trouble spreading his seed in good time." It was fun tormenting her mother. Her delicate sensibilities made her an easy target. Lexi picked up the remnants of her purse and Sawyer opened the squad car door for her. Once inside the silence was tense.

"So you said we needed to talk," she prompted.

"You gave away the flowers?" he questioned.

"Seriously... that's what you want to talk about?" she huffed crossing her arms in agitation.

"No, it isn't. But I don't know how to tell you what I need to tell you," he hesitated.

"Oh for the love of God, just spit it out. We are beyond being politically correct,"

"Raymond Brant escaped police custody last week and an FBI agent visited me this morning. He's concerned that Brant may try to harm you. Because of that, I'll be assigning someone to you until he's caught," he explained.

Well, shit.

Chapter 11

SAWYER

Lexi went stone cold at the mention of Brant's name. He was with Baxter when Jessica called. He heard part of the conversation and immediately went to find them. It was too big of a coincidence that Lexi would be involved in an incident the same day the FBI showed up to advise him of a threat. He didn't like it.

"Lexi, I need you to say something," he said.

"I can take care of myself, Sawyer," she gritted back.

For the love of all things good and great in the world...

"Lexi, you're getting protection whether you like it or not. If I need to I will personally sow me and you together, but you're not leaving my sight until this guy is caught," his voice was rough and commanding. If he used that tone with his Deputies, they would jump. Lexi just rolled her eyes, huffed and stared out the window.

They drove the rest of the way to Jenkin's Ranch in silence. He knew the conversation with Lexi would be difficult, he just never thought she would be stubborn enough to risk her life because she hated him. He would be the one to guard her, even if she hated the idea. He'd convinced her family that it was best. He planned to have security for Jack and the Scotts until the SOB was caught.

Lexi got out of the car and slammed the door. She was pissed, but he'd rather she be pissed than hurt. He followed her into the main house, where he knew there was about to be an exchange of words.

"Lexi, you need to trust me here," he said.

She turned around as she stood at the bottom of the stairs. She looked beautiful despite the gash on her head. Every time he saw her, it was as though she grew more and more attractive.

"I don't need a fucking babysitter, Sawyer!" she yelled. Her cheeks flushed and her hands moved dramatically in the air. She always was a hand talker. You always knew when she was pissed or excited about something.

"You do and I'm that babysitter! My job is to protect everyone in this county and that includes you!" he replied.

She crossed her arms over her delicious chest and he saw her grind her teeth from the doorway. She wasn't happy about the situation and who could blame her. He knew about their history and he knew she hated him. But he hoped that she could at least trust that he would do his job and protect her.

"Can't someone else do it?" she questioned.

Someone else? Why did she want someone else? He was the bloody Sheriff and the best person to keep her safe. He took a step forward.

"Is that a problem, Ms Scott?" he asked, clearly insulted that she didn't trust him to be responsible for her safety.

Lexi's mouth turned into a frown and her eyes shifted to everywhere except him. The pulse in her neck kicked up a couple of beats and he wondered if he made her nervous or if she was just pissed off.

"Yeah it's a problem," she said.

He took another step forward, but she didn't budge. Her sweet scent invaded his space as his breath sped up the closer he moved towards her. She always caused his body to react and she looked stunning when she was pissed at him. Life engulfed her face as her cheeks glowed and her eyes gleamed with fire.

"Why is it a problem Lexi?" he moved closer to her. He couldn't explain the draw he felt towards her and he sensed that she didn't want him around her because he would break through the walls she'd built to keep him out. And he wanted to demolish those damn walls. Walls he knew that he helped build because he was a stupid dick ten years ago.

"Because, it's you," she admitted.

He raised his hand to her nape and

caressed her jaw with his thumb. She didn't flinch or move away, and he just needed to touch her.

"I'm the best one to protect you, Lexi. I care what happens to you and I would never let anything hurt you," he whispered as they moved closer together. They were a magnetic force that despite their best efforts, they continued to pull towards each other.

When they were a breath apart, Lexi's shoulders sagged and her eyelids fluttered closed. She moved into his touch before she muttered a curse under her breath. She stepped up and brushed her soft perfect lips against his. She pulled back tentatively as if second-guessing her decision and stared at Sawyer.

"I-I'm so sorry. I don't know why... I shouldn't have..."

That was as far as she got before he dragged her into him and caught her lips with his. The electricity between them lit the fire that had burned fierce ten years ago. She melted into his arms with a sigh and his hand floated to her waist and tugged her closer to his body. He could feel the soft swipe of her breasts against his chest and the delicate curve of her back. She was never a super skinny woman, and he loved every inch of her curves. He wanted to kiss and appreciate every luscious inch of her body.

He tilted her head back to deepen the kiss and swiped his tongue over her bottom lip. She returned with a nip to his bottom lip before their tongue swam together in an intoxicating and hot kiss. He turned her so that her back was against the nearest wall and he continued to ravage her mouth. Her hands flew to his hips and she yanked him closer by slipping her fingers into his belt loops. He pushes his erection up against her, which caused a sexy moan to escape her lips.

He moved his kisses from her lips to worship the sweet taste of her skin. He suckled her nape, collar bone and returned to her ear lobe where he nibbled before he returned to her mouth. Their bodies ground against each other causing a throbbing sensation in his pants. He'd never been this turned on from a kiss with anyone else. He felt her dampness as her core rubbed against his erection.

His body remembered hers and she was always so responsive to his touch. The sound of a car coming up the drive startled them out of their impromptu make-out session with teenage dry humping. Lexi jumped back and put distance between them.

"That was a mistake," she mumbled before she ran upstairs and out of sight.

The best mistake he'd made lately. He took a minute to calm himself down and adjust his dick before whoever had arrived entered the house. He moved into the kitchen and turned on the coffee pot. He suspected the argument with Lexi about her protective detail was only starting and there would be more cussing and fighting in the future.

"Hey man," Jack said, as he entered the kitchen. He shook Jack's hand and pulled out two coffee mugs for them.

Jack had only been a kid when Lexi's accident happened, but Sawyer had made him promise back then not to upset Lexi by telling her that he was checking in on her. He didn't understand at the time, but since then Sawyer and Jack had become friends. Jack had stayed in Silverton and had no ambitions to seek the riches of the big city like Lexi had done.

They sat at the small breakfast nook while they waited for the coffee to be ready. Sawyer huffed and rubbed his brow. He was convinced that he would need Botox before this was over. Lexi seemed to cause a perpetual crease in his forehead.

"So, you and sis getting along as normal I see," Jack chuckled as he sat across from Sawyer.

"Jack, man, she's like a bull in a China shop. I don't even have to say anything and she's pissed off," Sawyer said as he leaned back in his chair. A smug smile crossed Jack's face as he got up to get the coffee.

"You'll get used to it," he shrugged. "She doesn't like being told what to do. The more you try and push her the farther away she's going to run," he commented.

"Have you talked to your folks about

what's been happening?" Sawyer asked. Jack nodded, but Sawyer wanted to make sure he knew how serious the threat to Lexi was.

"She hates the fact that I'm going to be protecting her. I'm the best person to do that and your parents agreed. I would sooner take a bullet than ever let anything hurt Lexi," Sawyer admitted.

Jack sipped his coffee and smiled before he responded, "You've been in love with my sister for as long as I can remember, McGuire. Unfortunately, the man you are now is paying for the crime he did to her heart when you were a stupid jackass."

Sawyer twisted his neck back and forth trying to release some tension in his shoulders. He knew Jack was right, but he had no idea how to go about making amends with Lexi. What he did was disgusting and he wished he could go back in time and fix it. But he couldn't.

"I don't even know where to start. I've tried, you know that. Every time she has returned to visit, I've tried. After a while, I guess I just gave up," he said.

Jack clapped him on the shoulder, "If you want what is best for Lexi, you need to tell her the truth about what happened after you were an eighteen-year-old jack-ass."

They sat together and chatted about Brant and how the Sheriff's department would be working to make sure everyone was safe from any possible threat. And then Lexi appeared and his mouth when dry. The sight standing before him was a threat to his sanity and resolve.

Chapter 12

LEXI

She must have hit her head harder than she originally thought. That was the only explanation for why she would be voluntarily sucking face with Sawyer at the bottom of her stairwell. What the fuck was she thinking? She had a lot of feelings about Sawyer and it confused the shit out of her. She tackled some of the most complex criminal cases but couldn't manage to sort through her emotional baggage and feelings towards the guy who took her virginity.

Fuck, it had been a rough day. Lexi knew Sawyer would keep to his word about ensuring that she didn't leave his sight until whatever potential threat he thought there was disappeared. She heard muffled voices through the door of the bathroom and determined that Sawyer was on the phone and was out on the front porch.

As quiet as possible she snuck down to the kitchen and grabbed a bottle of wine and a glass to bring upstairs with her. When she made it to the bathroom without another awkward encounter with the swoon-worthy cowboy Sheriff, she breathes a sigh of relieve. She locked the bathroom door and undressed as the water filled the soaker tub. She poured herself a generous glass of the 1993 Merlo and slipped into the warm water.

She did her best thinking in the bath and right now, she needed to do some thinking. Brant was out and Sawyer had reason to believe that he would target her. She thought that he was being paranoid about the incident with the car, but it was hard to convince him of something else once he'd made up his mind. She knew what she needed and she knew just the ladies to help her.

She reached over and grabbed her phone. She quickly sent a group message to Aubrey, Jordan and Daisy.

Lexi: I need a night out

Daisy: I know what that means!

Aubrey: I'm putting on my square-dancing boots. I haven't tested them out yet!

Jordan: I'll drop the kids off to Remi and Sawyer and we can meet up at the bar?

Lexi: Sawyer is here. Thus the reason I need a night out.

Daisy: I'm glad I ordered the fancy tequila from the vendor.

Aubrey: You sure a night is going to cut it? If I know Sawyer, you probably need a couple of weeks on a beach surrounded by beautifully bronzed cabana boys.

Jordan: Say no more. Meet you in an hour.

Lexi didn't have many friends back in New York and typically she found any kind of relationship difficult to maintain with her job. But she was in Silverton and if there was one thing the McGuires could do and do well, it was partying.

Lexi took her time getting out of the shower, she wrapped herself in a towel that still smelt like Nana before she made her way downstairs. She knew Sawyer would have to be made aware of her night out. Her hair was still wet and dangled down her shoulders and beads of water still dripped down her arms. She found Sawyer in the kitchen, talking to Jack. His gaze took in her lack of clothing and darkness settled in his eyes.

"Jesus Christ, can you put some clothes on before you go strolling through the house?" Jack hollered.

"Be grateful I'm wearing a towel little bro. When I'm in my condo I don't typically bother with it," she teased, and she swore a growl was heard from Sawyer and the vein on his forehead throbbed again.

"Sheriff, I know you've asked that there be protection assigned to me," she said.

"I think it would be best and we were just talking about that," he announced.

"Well, how nice of you two to talk about things that concern me without me present. Whomever you have scheduled to surveil this evening, please ask them to dress casually," she ordered.

Sawyer tilted his head as if questioning her authority. His beautiful bright green eyes narrowed before he asked, "Why?"

She shrugged, "I'm going out with some girlfriends to the Barn House and I would prefer if whoever is assigned not interrupt my fun. I've had a hell of a week and I want to unwind with some dancing, beers and cowboys."

Without waiting for a response, Lexi turned on her heel and climbed the stairs to her bedroom. There she blow-dried her hair, applied makeup, and picked out a sexy little black dress with some seductive red heels. Lexi used her hair to cover her scar. Some guys didn't feel comfortable talking to her because of it and others wanted to know everything about it. She was hoping that because it was Silverton that she could have a normal night since everyone already knew how she got the scars.

She sat on the end of her bed, slipping on her heels when her door flew open and a pissed-off looking Sheriff walked in and closed the door. His hands were sternly placed on his hips and his face dawned a 'don't mess with me' glare that she was sure scared half his deputies. It was a good thing she didn't find him intimidating.

"You're not leaving this house tonight," he directed, his tone held authority.

Lexi glanced up from where she was strapping on her heel and stood to face Sawyer. She would not be threatened, not by some psychotic serial killer, an asshole prosecutor or a sexy Sheriff. He didn't intimidate her. She had chewed up more criminals in her time than he had in his entire police career. She straightened out the front of her dress before she moved toward him. His gaze scrutinized every inch of her body and if it was even possible, his scowl deepened.

"Sheriff," she started in a calm, almost creepy voice, "am I under arrest for something?"

Before he answered, she interrupted, "No, I am not. Therefore there are no grounds by which you are to confine me to this residence. I will not have my life dictated by a serial killer and a Sheriff. I will be leaving this house in five minutes when my ride arrives. If you intend to be the one on shift this evening, then fine. We need a designated driver anyway."

She made to move past him to open the bedroom door and sneak out, but Sawyer caught her hand. His face had become gentle and relaxed. He held her hand and tugged her against his hard body. It wasn't fair that the man had to be the one she hated. He was too damn tempting and her feelings were jumping around like an unmedicated child with ADHD.

"Is this about what happened downstairs?" he asked.

She scoffed, "Contrary to your beliefs, Sheriff, not everything revolves around you. And it would take a hell of a kiss to get me to comply with your requests, that one was mediocre at best."

His face moved closer to hers as she glared at him with pure defiance. He was going to kiss her again and Lexi didn't know if her will power could handle another lip lock with him.

"I think it was more than mediocre, Lex," he whispered, his lips just a hair away from her lips. She could feel the soft breathe on her face and smell his earthy cologne.

"It's not going to happen again, Sheriff," she hissed, as she gritted out the last word before she slid out of his grasp and made her way downstairs. A groan was heard as she descended the stairs before loud footsteps followed behind her. In the driveway, Daisy sat on the hood of her car. Black hair blew in the wind and beautiful tattoos on full display. She stepped off the porch toward Daisy.

"Lexi!" Sawyer bellowed from the stoop.

"Are you coming or do you plan to change the laws on forcible confinement in the next thirty-seconds?" she goaded.

Sawyer pulled a hand down one side of his face and let out an unpleasant groan before heading towards Daisy's car. Daisy's smug grin told Lexi that she enjoyed watching someone outside their family take Sawyer down a notch.

"Well, big bro, are you ready for girls night?" Daisy asked sarcastically.

Sawyer mumbled something under

his breath that sounded like unfavourable cusses that her good southern mama would faint over. With a deepened scowl, he climbed in the driver's seat of Daisy's truck, automatically assuming the role of DD for the evening. Daisy looked amazing as always with her skin-tight black jeans, black tank and cowboy boots. She always wore her hair down around her face and her arms were bare most of the time showing off her tattoos. Jordan and Aubrey were next to pick up since Daisy reached her ranch before the McGuire's. Both ladies were dressed like supermodels and Aubrey gave Remi a hot kiss on the step before she left. She slid into the truck with a grin on her face.

"Jesus Aubrey, I think I might have gotten pregnant just watching that kiss," Daisy joked.

Aubrey huffed from the back seat as she reapplied her lipstick with a handheld mirror, "You sweet girl, need to get laid."

"Now now, Aubrey. Tonight isn't about me getting laid, it's about Lex getting laid," Daisy argued, with a mocking tone to her sultry voice.

Lexi didn't have to look at Sawyer to feel his glare burning holes into the side of her face. Lexi kept her eyes on the passenger side window as the ladies in the back talked about possible options for Lexi's one night plough.

"What about Finn?" Aubrey asked. Sawyer swerved sharply causing the truck to jolt before he readjusted.

"What about him?" Jordan questioned.

Aubrey rolled her eyes as though exasperated with her sister in law, "Well, I know Finn and Lex go way back and I happened to see them having coffee the other day and things looked to be heating up from where I was sitting."

The four heads invading the truck quickly whipped to Lexi. For fuck's sake, couldn't a girl just have coffee with a friend? But the glare from Sawyer made her think that he could be jealous of his younger attractive little brother. An evil thought crossed her mind and she decided she would play up her "attraction" to the younger McGuire to see what happens. She was convinced it would be like the time Jack tried to flush their house cat down the toilet, but what the hell.

Aubrey turned to look at the waiting vixens, and with a shrug, she commented, "Finn could be an option."

A mischievous smirk lit up Daisy's face as she caught on to what Lexi was doing. She gave Lexi a playful wink to let her know that she had no issues playing along with her little plan.

"I always thought you guys would make a cute couple," Jordan attested.

Daisy slipped out her cell phone while Jordan and Aubrey talked about how Lexi could seduce Finn. All the while, she could feel Sawyer's jealousy fill the air of the truck.

"There!" Daisy shouted excitedly. "Finn said he will meet us at the bar in a bit for a beer. He's excited to see... ahem... everyone," Daisy said with an eye toward Sawyer, whose frown deepened and his knuckles turned white from the hard grip he had on the steering wheel. Lexi's phone buzzed from her purse and she reached in to see a text from Finn and Daisy.

Daisy: Bro, I need your assistance.

Finn: How much bail do you need?

Daisy: You bailed me out once! ONCE. But no, not asking for me. Lexi needs your help pissing off Sawyer.

Finn: Pissing off Sawyer is what I live for, add in Lexi and you know I won't say no. What do you need?

Daisy: I need you to meet us at the bar in 20 and pretend you're interested in screwing Lex.

Lexi: Take a breath, Finn! It would be fake. But your brother has gone to new lengths to piss me off and I know how much you enjoy doing that to him. It would be completely fake.

Finn: Ladies, ladies... you don't need to convince me. I'm already out the door. See y'all soon. ;)

Aubrey tapped Lexi on the shoulder from behind, snapping her attention from her phone, "Who are you talking to that would make you smile like that Sexy Lexi?"

Lexi's groaned. She hated that nickname and would prefer anything other than Sexy Lexi. Especially since her scars make her feel anything but sexy.

"It was just Finn letting me know he was heading to the bar," she answered.

She was almost certain that Sawyer's face started to turn a bright shade of red as she released this bit of information. She was about to have some serious fun fucking with him. Payback was a bitch and she was about to handsome in bulk to the broody Sheriff who broke her heart.

Chapter 13

SAWYER

Sawyer pulled into the parking lot of the Barn House and hopped out of the car. Given the large area of the bar, he asked a couple of Deputies to help him surveil the location and wear civilian clothing to blend in with the crowd. He was already pissed and needed something to punch, so he hoped there was a brawl or an asshole who needed a bit of manhandling to help him out.

Finn. She was looking to get laid with Finn. He didn't know how he felt about that, considering Lexi had seen him walk out of the bar several times with one or sometimes two ladies. But his brother? No, that was the line that should not be crossed and Finn knew their history, there was no way he looked at Lexi as anything more than a friend.

After the perimeter had been secured and the guys were set up inside, Sawyer let the ladies hop out of the truck. As soon as they hit the gravel with their high heel shoes, Finn's truck pulled up next to them. He got out of his stupid ass truck wearing his best denim and a button-down. He immediately spotted Lexi and rushed to pick her up and spin her around as he hugged her. She laughed and he wished he'd been the one to draw that sound out of her. Along with a variety of other sounds.

"Hey there sweetheart!" he said, as he put her down on her feet but didn't release her. Instead, he guided her into a spin so he could take a peek at her outfit. "Damn, you look good enough to eat," he said with a wolf whistle.

Lexi blushed as she stopped in front of him, "That could be arranged if you play your cards right."

Sawyer was done with this shit and leaned against the hood of the truck, took his weapon out of his holster and cocked it to get everyone's attention. Sure enough, they all turned at the sound of his 9 mm.

"Y'all want to go inside or are you two just going to eye fuck right out here in public," he growled as he bit back his anger.

Finn's eyebrow raised and a slow smirk grew across his face as Lexi curled her arm around his waist.

"C'mon Sugar, I'm really looking forward to scuffing up that dance floor with you," Lexi cooed as she dragged Finn towards the entrance. Sawyer tried not to act like a homicidal maniac when he saw Finn's filthy paw roaming too close to Lexi's amazing ass. It looked too damn good in that dress.

A clap on the shoulder knocked him out of thought on how to bury his brother's body. The fierce little hand doled out a hardcore slap.

"How ya doing there big brother?" Daisy asked as she moved into the bar with the others. There was something fishy about the whole situation and if there was something amiss it involved the devils that were his sisters.

Sawyer was trying hard to maintain a sense of composure and professionalism. Especially since he was assigned to protect Lexi, but the woman was making it hard to fucking do that when she was being a fucking seductress.

Sawyer steadied himself and moved into the bar. His eyes immediately landed on his target and he checked in with the guys he had posted on the inside.   The bar was hopping and the smell of stale air and smoke sunk into his pores. He didn't know how his sister spent so much time in the shit hole, but she was his sister and they supported her.

Sawyer posted himself in the corner facing the door and within clear sightline of Lexi. As mad as he was that Finn was fawning over her, he also felt secure that Finn would never let anything happen to Lexi. He stood back and watched as the ladies drank and laughed with each other and others who gravitated towards them.

"How's it going baby bro?" Remi said as he shoved at Sawyer's shoulder. Sawyer eyed him curiously. He was supposed to be watching Jordan's youngsters tonight. Hopefully, no one would need medical attention in the county because the doctor was not in. Well, she was intoxicated and currently sucking face with some douche canoe from city hall.

"What are you doing here?" Sawyer asked.

"Miss Martha took the kiddos for a sleepover, so I figured I'd come to make sure the horn dogs stay away from my woman," he replied, his eyes falling to Aubrey as she threw her head back and laughed at something Daisy said. She was three sheets to the wind. Nothing Daisy ever said was that funny.

Aubrey was a beautiful woman, so he understood Remi's need to ensure all the dicks in the room knew not to mess with her. But there were still some fellas passing through who were charmed by the Canadian sweetheart. And who could blame them? Sawyer was proud to welcome her to the family and was delighted when his brother took the very large tree trunk out of his ass and realized his feelings for her.

"No offence, but I doubt Aubrey would need your help in that department. She's got a killer right hook," he smirked.

"Aint that the truth," Remi smiled widely as he raised his beer to his lips for a sip. "I prefer she has all the function of her right hand," he waggled his brow comedically as Sawyer rolled his eyes and groaned.

"You two are so adorable it's disgusting," Sawyer replied.

"Yep. But in other news, what's happening with Finn and your girl over there?" Remi lifted his beer in the direction of the couple. Finn had his right hand on her lower back and was bent into her as he whispered something in her ear.

"Don't know, don't care,"

"Have you told that to your face? Because right now if looks could kill, Finn would have been dead three times over,".

"I don't know what you're talking about," he replied, pulling his eyes from Finn and relaxing the fist he didn't know he'd made.

Remi turned to him and stood in his line of sight, blocking his view of the pair.

He had his "don't mess with me" brother face on and Sawyer could tell he was about to start preaching at him.

"Have you told her everything?" he asked and Sawyer shifted his eyes from his brother.

"I'll take that as a no. Why the hell haven't you told her everything you've done to change since that night?"

"Because it wouldn't make a God damn difference, Rem. She hates me and I broke her heart. And you know what, I deserve her hate. I was a dumbass kid who did stupid shit and never thought about how it could hurt her. None of us were the same after that night and as much as I wish I could turn back the clock and do it differently, I can't. And I can't get her to forgive me..." he sighed.

He realized at that moment that he would be a different person had it not been for the events of that night ten years ago. He'd always known who Lexi was and always noticed her. But he cared too much about his reputation and popularity when he was in high school. It was hard walking in the same halls as the great Remington McGuire.

Holding Lexi in his arms the night of her accident shifted his entire world. After she ran from the party, he chased her. He saw the hurt and pain pool in her eyes as she fought back the tears. He knew he had made a terrible mistake. Of all the people who made fun of her, he should've known better. He ran for her, but he didn't reach her in time. He watched as a black car hit her and her body rolled and hitched on the back of the car. The driver never slowed and he chased after the car as Lexi's screams rang through the air.

Once she had untangled from the car, he rushed for her. She was unconscious, bloody and pale. Her eyes were closed and she winced when he held her. The deep jagged slice down her beautiful face bled over his clothing and he took off his shirt, trying to slow it. When the ambulance and police arrived, he drove with her to the hospital. Never letting go of her hand.

All he thought about was how horrible he had been to her. How he may never get the chance to make it right, to apologize, to tell her how he felt. He refused to let go of her hand until she was wheeled into the ER operating room. He sat in the waiting room for eight hours while they operated and tried to control her internal bleeding.

The next day, he enlisted in the Army.

Sawyer shook the thoughts from him and he stared back at his brother. He must have seen the pain on his face because his features softened and he clapped Sawyer's shoulder.

"You're a good man, Sawyer," Remi said before Aubrey's body rushed into his in a fierce hug.

"What are you doing here?" she squealed in delight.

"I couldn't stay away, darling. As soon as you left the house in that dress, I was a goner," he pulled her closed and kissed her.

Sawyer looked around for Lexi and found her behind the bar with Daisy offering free shots. Lexi had several drinks in her system when a seductive slow dance came on from Pistol Annies, *"I feel a sin coming on"*. She yanked on Finn's hand and dragged him onto the dance floor. They began a typical slow dance and Finn kept a respectable distance. But Lexi wasn't feeling that and turned so her ass was grinding up against his hips. Finn's hands fell to her hips as she twisted and swayed her curves against his body.

That was it. He was done. Rage burned in his eyes as he zoned in on his target. Before he knew what he was doing, he'd made his way to the dance floor and stood in front of the couple. He bored holes into his brother before he spoke.

"You. Go. Now," Sawyer commanded.

Finn was a smart man and he quickly raised his hands off Lexi's hips and stepped back. The smile on his face continued to grow as he walked farther towards the bar where the girls were drinking. Leaving him to face a pissed off Lexi, who'd had one too many tequila shots, for him to deal with.

He grasped her wrists and pulled her

towards the rear exit where they could speak privately. She rolled her eyes as he dragged her along. He felt eyes digging into the back of his head. He pushed the door open with force and slammed it behind them. Lexi made her way across the alley and leaned against a brick wall.

"What the heck, Sawyer?"

"What the fuck do you think you're doing with my brother?" he snapped.

She crossed her arms over her chest, causing her breast to push up high revealing the sultry curve of her mounds. "I was having a good time! What did it look like I was doing?"

"It looked like you were about to fuck my brother on the dance floor!" he gritted.

She raised one of her brows as her stare narrowed on him, "What does it matter to you who I fuck!?" she screamed back and he could see her heart beating wildly in her chest. She was enjoying this. And then it hit him. She was trying to make him jealous.

Well, congratulations, it worked.

He held her stare as he strode quickly towards her, "If you're going to fuck a McGuire, Lexi. It's going to be me and only me," he spat, as his body pinned her in place against the wall. He spied goosebumps crawl up her arms as she heard his words. She was turned on and he wanted her that way.

Without any warning, Lexi's hands yanked the nape of his neck towards her and forced her lips to his with a groan. He kissed her back with the viciousness and desperation of a starved man. Her hot tongue ploughed into his mouth and covered his lips in her sweet taste. God, he couldn't get enough of her and he wanted to taste every inch of her.

But he wouldn't.

He couldn't.

Reluctantly, he yanked himself away from Lexi. She deserved better than him and he knew it. She deserved someone who hadn't already broken her heart and caused her pain. He couldn't look at the scar without feeling regret that he couldn't prevent her pain. He shook his head and closed his eyes.

"I can't," he whispered.

Lexi's breathing slowed and she smoothed out her skirt before turning on her heel and walking back into the bar. He needed to get his head on straight so he strutted into the bar and approached his brother and the deputies.

"I need you to do something for me," he said to Finn.

"Depends on what it is, brother," he smirked.

"I need you to stay with Lexi tonight and until I arrive tomorrow morning. The deputies here will be standing guard outside the house, but I want someone I trust on the inside with her."

Finn's face dropped and his brow scrunched together in confusion. Sawyer handed him the car keys and without a second glance, exited the Barn House. He was just going to hurt her more if he was close to her. He needed to keep her safe, not break her heart all over again.

Chapter 14

LEXI

Lexi sat on the cold toilet seat in a small stall of the ladies bathroom. She needed a moment to get her shit together before she had to face Sawyer. She wanted to hate the man. She really wanted to hate everything about him. But she couldn't. She needed to apologize to him and she needed to stop making his job more difficult than it needed to be.

She was getting ready to open the stall when the door to the ladies room flew open and two female voices flooded the room.

"Can you believe she thinks Finn is into her?" One female scoffed.

"I know right! As if anyone could find her attractive with that ugly scar on her face. She wasn't pretty before, but now, she's just a monster," the other commented.

Lexi peered through the small opening in the stall to catch a glimpse of the girls who were about to get their asses kicked. Both bleached blond. Typical. Their skirts were so tight that they looked like overstuffed sausages. Not to mention you could see what they had for breakfast if they bent the wrong way. Lexi had spent far too long trying to love herself and she wouldn't let two space cadets tarnish her confidence or intimidate her.

With that, she opened the door and eyed the girls in the mirror. Both of their eyes widened when they spotted Lexi. Without a word, Lexi made her way to the sink, where she washed and dried her hands while keeping an eye on the women before her. Both of them diverted their gaze, proving to Lexi that besides being rude, they were also cowards. It was easy for people to talk behind someone's back, but the cowards would never do it to their face.

Lexi kept a big smile on her face the

whole time and as she left the restroom, she hauled open the door before glancing back at Mandy and Candy.

"If I ever see either of you within twenty feet of a McGuire man, I will ensure that you will be sorry. Not that the McGuires would slump so low as to risk an STD by shacking up with the town bicycles," she lashed as she walked out the door.

Why people felt the need to constantly poke fun at her for something she could not control, she wouldn't know? She couldn't change the scar on her face or the past that created it. But it'd be a cold long day in hell before she'd let those two insult her.

Lexi reached Aubrey and Jordan who sat at the bar while Finn and Daisy did some line dancing. Her eyes searched for Sawyer, with no success. She slid up to the girls and grabbed a beer while she watched the people on the floor dancing.

"Where's the annoying Sheriff?" Lexi asked.

"He left," Aubrey responded.

Left?

What happened to the straight-talking cop who was dedicated to her protection?

"Where'd he go?" She asked.

Aubrey shrugged and took a sip of her beer. "I believe he went home," Aubrey was wrapped in the embrace of Remi from behind and he dragged her out onto the dance floor. They were so in love it was sickening. As much as she didn't want that connection with someone, she found herself feeling jealous of them. She would struggle to find someone who had the balls to go on a second date with her after seeing her scar, for the rest of her life.

Jordan turned her back to Lexi as she chatted up some young buck from City Hall. Newfound anger formed in her chest at the thought that Sawyer left her after his big speech on ensuring her safety.

She grabbed her purse off the chair and slipped on her jean jacket. She snuck out of the bar without much issue and was able to call a cab. Of course, the cab was nothing like what you would expect to see in Manhattan. No, the cab was driven by Earl, who coincidentally also drove the school bus. Earle was a kind older man, who had lost his wife several years ago to Cancer. He'd always been kind to her and she appreciated all the kindness she could get after the accident. Lord knew she was hard enough on herself, she didn't need others degrading her.

"Hey Earl," Lexi greeted as she slid into the passenger side of the painted green minivan.

"Howdy Darling. Long time no see there Lex. You heading back to your folks' house?" Earl was a jolly man who had a distinct resemblance to Santa Claus. He had a long white shaggy beard and piercing blue eyes and a kind soul.

The ride back to Jenkin's ranch was quiet and Lexi debated sending Sawyer a text or letting Jordan know that she'd left. When Earl pulled up to the gate of her ranch and went to get out to open the gate, she stopped him. She was fine to walk the half-mile to the main house. Earl was hesitant to do so and refused to let her pay him.

Lexi watched as the green minivan's brake lights faded in the distance. She went to the old tacky mailbox and opened the door to check the mail. She walked as she shifted quickly through her mail until one particular envelope caught her attention. There was no return date and no stamp to indicate it was mailed the regular way.

She ripped the seam and opened the letter. Using the flashlight from her phone she unwrapped the sheet of paper. Her step faltered and her heart stopped. Her body began to shake and she quickly searched her surroundings to see if anyone lurked in the darkness. She yanked off her pepper spray from her key chain and did what she didn't want to do. She ran. She grasped her fingers tightly around the letter as she sprinted to the house, refusing to look behind her in case she lost her resolve.

Once she reached the house, she slammed the door shut and locked the deadbolts. She tried hard to breathe before she punched in a phone number to call for help. She called the only person she knew would know what to do at that moment.

"Hello?" Sawyer's gruff voice radiated through the other end of the phone. She tried to regain her breath before she spoke, but a sob left her before she could stop it.

"Sawyer..." she gasped.

"Lexi, what's wrong? Where are you?" Sawyer asked, as she heard clothing tussle in the background. She'd woken him.

"Sawyer, it's Brant. I need you at the ranch now," she plead.

"Stay on the phone Lexi. Don't hang up, you hear me? No matter what don't hang up," his voice was frantic and she heard him get into his truck as she struggled to maintain her composure. She heard a car come up the drive, and Sawyer yelling that it was him.

Lexi rose from the floor, the note still crumpled in her shaking hands as she twisted the deadbolt to let Sawyer into her home. The door swung open and Sawyer grabbed her shoulders and examined her.

"What's wrong?" he asked, the compassion flowed through his tone. With that, he pulled her into his arms and held her as she sobbed uncontrollably.

"Lexi, sweetheart, you need to tell me what's going on," he asked calmly, as his warm palm circled her back in soothing motions.

Lexi offered him the crumpled paper as she took a step back from him. Her hands continued to shake and the level of pity that glowed in Sawyer's eyes hit the core of her heart.

Sawyer pulled open the letter and read aloud the contents.

"You can run, but you can't hide, my pet. I've saved the best for last and I'm coming to collect. See you soon, Brant."

"Where did you get this?" He asked.

Everything around her slowed and her eyes fixated on a spot on the floor. Her breathing came hard and rough as the taste of her tears flooded her mouth. She stumbled backwards and made towards the head of the couch to sit. Her legs trembled and sweat had begun to drip down the back of her neck.

He was here. He was planning to kill her. What did he mean by saving her for last? What was happening to the others who put the bastard away? Surely, he didn't mean... Lexi's shaky hand flew to her mouth as she gasped.

"No..." And then all the air left her lungs and all she could see was black engulfing the corners of her vision. Her body felt light and her energy faded. She felt her body slump and she had no control as she tumbled. But rather than hitting the hard floor, she was wrapped in strong secure arms.

"Shit!" Sawyer mumbled, as he pulled her into his arms and carried her bridal style up the stairs. Lexi's head rested on his chest and she concentrated on the gentle beat of his heart and it calmed her. He kicked open the bedroom door and gently laid her on the bed before he sat alongside her.

"Lexi," he said, his voice soft and concerned. Lexi looked up and saw the lines of fear etched across his handsome features. He was worried about her. He gently grazed her cheek with the back of his knuckles, leaving a path of fire in their wake. She closed her eyes as she embraced his touch with a sigh.

"Stay with me," she asked, "please, Sawyer. I can't be alone right now and I'll feel safer with you here."

"You would need a tractor to haul me out of here right now, Lexi. I'm going to call those dumb asses who lost you at the bar and get them to secure the perimeter. Are you okay? I should call Jordan and get her to check you out," he said, as he stood and paced the front of the bed.

Lexi sat up on the bed and took a deep breath to ground herself, but the shaking in her hands still radiated through her body.

"I'm fine Sawyer," she said. She wasn't sure if she was trying to convince him or herself. He turned and caught her eye and the anger that flared in his emerald eyes stirred a fire deep inside her.

"You are not fine, Lexi!" he bellowed as he stalked towards her, his strong hands rested on his hips and his "Sheriff's face" switched up to high gear. "Those idiots couldn't even keep you safe for one night!"

He raked his fingers through his light brown locks and she wondered if it was as soft as she imagined and how it would feel to run her fingers through it.

"Sawyer..." she tried to interrupt, but he was fired up and ready to go.

"No Lexi, I know you hate me, but I don't care. I'm going to be stuck to your side until this psycho is back behind bars where he belongs, you hear me?"

He thought she hated him. She'd been confused about her feelings for the scowling man standing in front of her, but she never hated him. Not really... She may have said that a time or two, but she knew the truth. She loved everything about him and she never stopped. When she first saw him in the Sheriff's office wrapped around some dingbat, she was jealous. She didn't want him to see through the mask she had prepared, so she resorted to the ice queen facade.

She rose from the bed and walked towards him until she could see the rapid rising of his chest with his breath. They stood there, an inch apart as their eyes bored into each other and Lexi felt a part of her soul get lost in the emotion in his eyes. She raised her hand to subtly caress his hard, strong jaw that was covered in stubble. His eyes closed on contact and he leaned into her hand.

"I've never hated you, Sawyer," she confessed in a soft voice.

At that moment, she knew it to be true and hearing it come from her lips only solidified the feelings in her heart. As much as Sawyer hurt her a decade ago, she could no longer hold him prisoner. She could no longer live her life without the risk of losing her heart again. She saw for the first time, that a heart that's been broken, was a heart that loved and been loved.

"Lexi…" he started with an exasperated breath and she already knew he was going to argue with her. But she wouldn't allow it. She moved her fingers to cover his mouth and when she moved them away allowed her thumb to slowly graze his full bottom lip.

"Don't…" she plead, as her eyes zeroed in on his lips.

She knew when she was seventeen that Sawyer McGuire was the one who could break her heart. She knew it the moment she laid eyes on him. The night of the accident her life had been shattered, but she found the strength to move forward. To relearn all the things she'd already managed. Of all the things she needed to teach herself again, loving Sawyer was never one of them. Despite the hurt and the betrayal, she always loved him and he always held a piece of her with him.

She closed the gap between them and raised on her toes as she eased her lips onto his in a sweet tentative kiss. When she slowly pulled back she expected to see him ready to walk away or with pity tossed across his strong masculine features. Instead, she saw desire, heat and a raw passion grow as he contemplated his next step.

She stepped back and out of his embrace as she realized his hesitation. Now was not the time to rekindle whatever happened between them. He could never give her what she wanted. A house. A marriage. Kids and a dog. He was the perpetual playboy of Silverton and she had a scarred body and a wounded heart.

She felt the rising of heat in her cheeks as her embarrassment became clear.

"I-I'm sorry. I shouldn't have…" she whispered.

She had no time to react as Sawyer grasped her elbow and turned her towards him to capture her lips in a passionate kiss. She melted into the feel of his hard body pushed against her as his calloused hands dug into her waist, keeping her firmly where he wanted her.

The kiss intensified as her hands floated to wrap around his neck and she nipped at his bottom lip. With a growl, he gripped her tighter to him and opened his mouth to her tongue. She moaned in delight as their tongues danced together in a perfect storm of sexuality and angst. She wanted him in every way humanly possible. Sawyer pulled back and rested his forehead on hers as they panted.

"Don't ever apologize for kissing me," he said, as a small smile crept across his lips.

"Stay with me, Sawyer," she begged, as she fisted his shirt and bit her bottom lip nervously in anticipation.

"Okay, Lex. Whatever makes you comfortable. But I'll take the floor," he said with a wink, as he made his way out of the bedroom to check all the other areas and secure all the entrances. Lexi ran to the doorway, baffled that she'd asked him to stay and he said he would. But on the floor?

"The floor? The bed is big enough for both of us," she argued. Sawyer stopped and turned on the stairs, piercing her soul with forest green eyes that blazed over her body.

"As much as I would love to darling, there are some things we should talk about before this," he motioned between them, "goes any further."

Her shoulder slumped at his rejection and she felt the sting of his words. Of course, he didn't want her. She was the girl with the scar. The "she would be pretty if it wasn't for that scar" girl. He must've recognized her line of thought because he sauntered to her and put his strong hands on the sides of her face raising her lips to his. He pressed a chaste kiss to them and he pulled away far too soon for her liking.

"I want you, Lexi. I want to keep you in that bed for days as I make your body scream my name over and over again. But we need to clear the air first," he said, as he placed a peck to her cheek and made his way down the stairs.

What the hell did he mean by clearing the air.

Chapter 15

SAWYER

Sawyer was on high alert and he needed reinforcements to ensure that Lexi stayed safe until Brant was re-captured. Once he secured all the locks on the doors, windows and checked every nook and cranny of the house, he pulled out his phone and called his brother.

"Please tell me you have Lexi?" Remi asked, his tone frantic and strained.

"Well, at least someone noticed she'd slipped out. Where the heck was the undercover?" Sawyer demanded, his voice rose in anger. What was the point of paying Deputies to serve and protect if they couldn't follow simple orders? He did not doubt that they were distracted by a short skirt and barely there shirt.

"Jesus, Sawyer. I have no idea. Me

and Aubrey have been searching the bar for thirty minutes for her. Do you have her?" Remi questioned.

"Yeah, I have her. But I need you, Jack, Finn and the ladies to come to Jenkin's ranch. I need your help."

"What's going on Sawyer?" Remi whispered into the phone as not to cause alarm to those who were around him.

"There have been some developments and I want everyone impacted here in my line of vision," Sawyer answered.

Remi sighed before he replied, "Okay brother. I'll grab the clan and get there at once. However, you should know… the ladies are pretty tanked."

The last thing he wanted to do for the remainder of the night was listen to Daisy and Jordan rant about how he ruined their fun again. Those two were a force when they were sober. Intoxicated and with his new sister in law… well, that was a recipe for disaster.

Sawyer groaned, "Jesus… Well, it's not like we can change that now, can we?"

Remi laughed at his brother's distraught and sarcastic tone, "Now, now brother, girls just wanna have fun, ya know? I'll get them there on the double. See ya soon."

Sawyer tossed his phone on the couch and cupped the back of his neck. He felt the tension forming in his shoulders and the stress of the day lodged in the curve of his back. He couldn't think about that now, he had to make sure that Lexi and everyone he loved was protected. He shot a text to the Deputy assigned to her parents and confirmed they were fine and still under surveillance. Luckily the Deputy was Parker and he was diligent about his duties. With that completed, he drew all the curtains in the house and went back upstairs to check on Lexi.

It wasn't an ideal time to have a chat with her about the past, but he had no choice if he wanted to build a relationship of some sort with her. He needed to divulge all the details to her so that she could make her own decisions.

He knocked softly on the door frame as he observed her sitting at an antique vanity brushing her long brown hair. Her gaze lifted and their eyes met in the mirror before she turned to face him. She'd changed into different clothes while he was downstairs and he inwardly groaned at her choice of attire. She wore a silky purple nightgown with lace covering the tops of her breasts and a matching robe. When she stood his eyes hungrily took in the short nightgown and the slim toned legs that were exposed.

She was testing his resolve. And the smirk that crossed her face when she caught his gaze, told him that she knew it.

She cleared her throat, "You said we needed to clear the air, Sheriff?".

Right. Clear the air.

He nodded before he gestured for her to take a seat next to him on the bed. He grasped her hands in his hands and brushed a kiss across her knuckles before he started. He inhaled deeply and reminded himself that the only way to move forward was to acknowledge the past. No matter how much it hurt.

"The night of the accident..." he

started. He physically felt Lexi's body posture tighten at the mention of the night that changed everything.

"Sawyer... I don't think we need to rehash the past..." she argued, as Sawyer shook his head.

"The truth is Lexi that I've waited a long time to talk with you about that night and I need to get it off my chest if there is ever going to be a future between us," he admitted.

Her brows furrowed and a crease formed two deep lines just above her nose. He could tell that she was thinking hard about what he said and reluctantly nodded for him to continue.

"We both know what happened before you left the party. And I'll be the first to admit I was a jackass. I never should have said those things about you. It was unfair. Especially, when my feelings for you were the opposite..."

Her eyes filled with unshed tears and his heart broke. He knew it was hard for her to remember that night, but he had to continue.

"But when you left the party so upset, I ran   after you," Sawyer admitted.

"W-What?" Lexi whispered as the shock and surprise caressed her beautiful face. She had no idea and no memory of what happened.

"I was maybe a block behind you when you stepped off the curb and the car hit you," his voice choked at the last word, as he recalled the devastation he felt as he saw Lexi's lifeless body sprawled across the pavement.

"When I got to you, you were in bad shape. There was a lot of damage and you were in and out of consciousness," he squeezed her hand tightly in his. He needed to touch her to remember that she made it out of that incident alive.

"Y-You were there?" she questioned.

"Yes. I was the first one there and Lexi I know that night changed everything for you. But at that moment, everything about who I was and who I wanted to be changed. Holding you in my arms as you bled and not knowing if you were going to be okay... that changed me," Sawyer's eyes stung as he fought back tears. He wasn't afraid to cry. Some people thought real men didn't cry, but he thought the opposite. Lexi's gaze met his as she raised her hand to brush a rogue tear from his cheek.

"Keep going. I want to know," she said softly.

He sniffed and caught her hand in his as he placed a delicate kiss to the inside of her palm.

"I refused to leave you and I rode with you to the hospital. I met your parents and brother and explained what had happened. After you came out of surgery and were permitted visitors, I visited. Almost every day for two weeks," he admitted. "But you were in a lot of pain and were in and out most of the time. When your parents took you to Houston, Jack kept me up to date on how you were doing," he said.

"Why hasn't anyone mentioned this to me before, Sawyer?" she asked.

"Because I asked them not to," he said guiltily, as he broke eye contact and stared at his feet. He couldn't look at her when he admitted that he didn't want her to know.

"Why?" She asked. Sawyer closed his eyes and grimaced as he continued with his story.

"One night when I was visiting, your parents and Jack had gone home for some much-needed rest and I agreed to stay with you. It was the night before you were to leave for Houston and I knew I wouldn't be able to see you once you left. I slept in the chair in the room and woke that morning to you yelling. You were screaming and crying in your sleep. I rushed over to try and soothe you. You must've woken a little bit and recognized me because you weren't happy."

"How do I not remember any of this? What did I say, Sawyer?"

"You told me that you would never forgive me and that I was the reason you were hurt. I was the reason your life would never be the same again and that you wanted me to leave you alone," he said, tears freely fell from his eyes as he recalled the hurt and pain he saw on her face back then.

Lexi gasped as her hand flew to her mouth. She knelt before him and stare at him as though she was peering into the unknown depths of his soul.

"I'm sorry Sawyer. I'm so so sorry. I didn't know... I- I," she sobbed before he pulled her into his arms.

"I don't blame you for feeling that way, Lex. But after that, I was determined to be a different person. I never wanted to make someone feel like that ever again. So the next day, I enlisted in the Army instead of taking that football scholarship to Texas State," he kissed the top of her head as she wrapped her arms around his neck.

"As horrible as that time was, it sent me on a path to become the man I am today," he said. "and I owe that to you, Lexi."

She raised her head from his chest and wiped the tears from his face.

"I was so wrong about you. I'm sorry. Please forgive me. I should have followed my heart a long time ago, but my pride stood in the way. I never meant to push you away. But I was afraid to pull you close as I wanted," she paused. "And I wanted to, Sawyer. I wanted you so badly that it hurt to see you."

"Do you still want that Lexi? Because I still want you and not just physically. I want it all Lex. The house. The kids. The wedding. The whole kit and caboodle. There has never been a woman who has made me want that besides you," he confided.

He knew he was getting a bit ahead of himself. He hadn't even asked her on a date, let alone fast forward to marriage and kids. But when it came to Lexi, he couldn't hold back his feelings. His heart wouldn't let him do it any longer.

"How's about we start with forgiving each other and maybe a date before we rush to the courthouse for a marriage license?" she smiled.

"Deal," Sawyer said before he grabbed her face and kissed her fiercely. He would never get enough of her. She was it for him and he knew it.

She wrapped her hands around his

neck and pushed him back onto the bed before she settled her thighs around his waist.

He could get used to this, he thought.

He ran his hands through her silky hair and devoured her. She moaned as his tongue ravished her sweet mouth and took its time to discover what she liked. His arousal grew and the zipper of his pants began to strain as her hardened nipples pressed into his chest. He growled and shifted positions. She yelped as he tossed her back on the bed and pinned her hands above her head and his hips between her thighs.

He moved his hand down her arm and briefly grazed her breast before gripping her ass in his palm. She whimpered and her body arched into him. With the little nightgown and panties the only barrier between his erection and her core, he felt her wetness as she rubbed her core against him.

"Oh, God…" she whispered against his lips, as he moved his hips to match her rhythm. His mouth moved down her nape, leaving open-mouthed kisses over her collar bone before taking a perky nipple into his warm mouth through her nightgown. Her hands flew his hair as she held him close to her.

"More, Sawyer, please…" she pleads as he moved from one perfect mound to the other. Sawyer was about to give in when there was a knock at the door. He groaned as rested her forehead against her shoulder.

"Who the hell is knocking on my door at 3 am?" she questioned. Sawyer peeled his body off of hers with great determination before he took her lips in a sweet kiss.

"My family…" he admitted.

"Talk about a cock block…" she joked before she moved around Sawyer to go answer the door. He grasped her elbow and pulled her into him.

"Perhaps you should put some clothes on first," he said.

She raised her eyebrow in challenge, "I rather like what I'm wearing, Sheriff."

He growled and kissed her again, "As do I. Very, very much. But I don't need my brothers seeing you in this. I want that for myself."

"Fine, fine, I'll change," she conceded before pressing a kiss to his cheek and turning towards the bathroom. As she strutted away from him, she pulled off the nightgown and dropped the robe, revealing her bareback and perfect little ass covered in a tiny piece of underwear. She looked over her shoulder before she said, "You better go answer the door Sheriff."

He closed his eyes tightly and chastised himself for bringing his family there. Now, he had to deal with them while trying not to picture Lexi naked and writhing under him.

"Fucking cock blocking family" he muttered, as he made his way out of the room.

Chapter 16

LEXI

Lexi sat in the living room curled up under a handmade throw her Nana made. She watched in awe as the people around her lost their shit. Aubrey was passed out on the love seat, Jordan was throwing up in the half bath and Daisy was yelling at Finn for something. It was a shit show. Meanwhile, Lexi barely kept her eyes open and her body screamed to take a nice long hot shower before she hopped into bed.

A loud whistle boomed through the room, which caught everyone's attention. Sawyer stood with his hands firmly placed on his hips as he finally got the attention of his family.

"Okay, y'all need to stop everything and listen..." he said sternly.

"Lex, perhaps you should start by telling us about Brant and his MO?" He said turning his stare toward her. The concern that flushed through his face only made her heart melt.

Lexi sat up and braced herself to relay the horrific details of Brant and her ongoing "friendship". Brant was a different kind of psycho. He got off on making others suffer the most and he reviled in pain. Lexi cleared her throat. She hadn't been able to get through talking about the victims without crying, but she wouldn't let herself do that in front of the McGuires.

"I worked with the DA in New York and I put a lot of scum behind bars for the rest of their lives. Brant was by far the only one that scared me. And with good reason. He murdered twelve young women in and around the New York area and dumped most of their bodies in prominent tourist attraction for others to find," she said.

Sawyer picked up on her discomfort and sat next to her on the couch. He grabbed her hand and intertwined their fingers before he squeezed tightly. She didn't know if he knew the magnitude of the gesture and that it gave her the strength to continue.

"And you were assigned the case?" Finn asked as he slouched against the door frame.

"Yes. Actually... I volunteered to take it," she admitted.

"Why?" Daisy countered.

Lexi took a deep breath before she worked up the nerve to continue. "The DA office in Manhattan is one of the largest and by far the biggest boys club. Women rarely went up in the ranks and I felt I had to prove myself. As a woman, I was seen as weak, but even I knew that having a female prosecutor on this case would make an impact on a jury," she confessed.

"Throughout the trial, which was an open and shut case. We had DNA and Brant was so narcissistic that he wanted all the glory for his murders," she scoffed, "Still, I was surprised when his attorney put him on the stand. It was a stupid move on their part, but I suspect Brant wanted the opportunity to take advantage of the limelight.

And I was right."

"What did he do to them, Lexi?" Jordan asked hesitantly. Lexi knew she wanted answers. God knew that Lexi had begged God many times while she cried over the photos of the victims, for answers.

"He kidnapped and murdered twelve women. The women all died from heart failure due to shock as Brant enjoyed torture. Each victim was tortured in many different ways before they ultimately succumbed to their injuries. The youngest victim was only fourteen."

By the time she'd taken on Brant, she had several wins under her belt. But she was never as impacted on any other file. She closed her eyes and saw their faces. A white sheet folded neatly over their collarbones while they lay on a cold hard slab of metal. She tried not to remember them that way. But the mind had an unusual way of working.

"During cross-examination, I didn't hold back. It wasn't about Brant. It was about the victims and I made sure that he knew that," she said firmly, as her memory of the cross-examination floated into her mind.

"Your witness, Ms Scott," the judge had bellowed in her direction.

Lexi stood and buttoned over her blazer. Brant hadn't taken his eye off her the whole trial and she wouldn't let him intimidate her. She knew just how to push his buttons and she wasn't going to stop until she did. She strode confidently towards the witness box, where Brant sat smugly after telling in disgusting detail what he did to his victims.

"Mr Brant, I'd like to first thank you," she announced.

"For what, Ms Scott?" he asked bemused.

"Well, you've made my job pretty easy," she smirked, "you've spent a lot of time telling the juror in extraordinary detail, all the horrors you inflicted on your victims. Are you proud of what you've done?"

The corner of Brant's mouth twitched.

"Of course I'm proud. Who wouldn't be proud of doing something exceptional to another?"

"We've heard you talk about what you've done to them," she stated as she slammed down twelve pictures in front of him of his victims and called out their names.

"Jane House."

SLAM

"Wendy Stratton"

SLAM

"Alyssa Barrington"

SLAM

"Jackie Sutherland"

SLAM

Jessica Degraw"

SLAM

"Ashley Barlow"

SLAM

"Melissa Foster"

SLAM

"April Flynn"

SLAM

"Judith Moores"

SLAM

"Brend La Croix"

SLAM

"Danielle Buckingham"

SLAM

"Janice Ryan"

SLAM

She never took her eyes off him as she finished her display and gathered the pictures. He didn't even deserve to look at them.

"But what about what was done to you, Mr Brant?"

His face dropped and his body tensed. The defence hadn't thought to dig into his history to identify any mitigating circumstances, but she had. She knew why he killed the way he did. She knew him better than she knew herself at that stage.

"Nothing was done to me…" he growled.

"On the contrary, Mr Brant. You see, when I take a case I like to get to know my opposition. You told everyone that you had perfect upbringing. That there was never any conflict and that you taught yourself how to kill, isn't that correct?"

He didn't answer.

"Tell me, Mr Brant, do you know a woman by the name of Maggie Branton?"

Silence.

"Oh c'mon, Mr Brant... You can't tell me that you don't know the name of your own mother," Lexi poked.

"She's not my mother," he gritted.

The doors at the rear of the court opened and in walked Maggie Branton, shackled and sporting an orange jumpsuit.

"There she is," Lexi commented.

"What the fuck is she doing here?" he screamed.

Lexi gave the guards a wave of her hand and they escorted Maggie out of the courtroom. Just her presence set off Brant.

"Now, would you like to revisit the question about your upbringing, or should I just continue and fill in the blanks for you?"

More silence.

"You see, your birth name is Branton. Your biological mother also happens to be one of the nation's most prolific serial killers. She could give Aileen Wurnous a run for her money," she paused, "But that's not all she did, is it Brant?"

She saw the pulse throb in his neck and his pupils contracted as his fists clenched for control.

"In fact, you were her first victim," she continued.

"I was not a victim!" he screamed.

"Oh yes you were and you have the scars to prove it. Cigarette burns on your arms, a tactic used on all of your victims. Whip marks on your back, also used by you. A hammer was taken to your kneecaps and hands..."

"STOP IT! You bitch! I did all of it! Not her. She's not going to steal my lime-light. I did everything and I'm a better killer than her!" he cried furiously.

Lexi closed the distance between her and him and stared him down.

"The only difference between you and your mother is that she got caught be-fore she could go past victim number ten. Otherwise, you're just a pitiful boy trying to be like his mommy."

Lexi jumped back into her reality and stared at the shocked and sad faces of the McGuires. Tears streamed down her cheeks, as they always did when she recounted slamming the victims' photos down.

"During the trial, I received various notes from Brant. Once he was placed in maximum security they stopped. It was symbolic to him. The only way we knew the murders were connected was because he stapled or nailed a note into the chest of his victims."

"Jesus Christ…" Remi said.

"Lex, what did the notes say?" Sawyer asked.

"Like this one," she nodded to the paper in his hand, "he referred to all his victims as his pet. Then he detailed their torture and deaths before taking responsibility and taunting the police."

"Brant escaped during transport and the FBI suspects he is hunting Lexi. Which is why I've called you all. Brant isn't above using the people Lexi loves to get what he wants. You all need to be on your game and cautious. I'm going to be staying here with Lexi but I need to know I can count on you guys to help if needed," Sawyer said.

Everyone around the room nodded.

"So, is everyone staying here or

what? I don't know about you guys but I need to sleep..." Lexi announced.

"Naw, I'm going to take the ladies home and have everyone stay at the ranch until this is over with. We don't want Emma and Leo in the middle of this," Remi stated.

The crew stood and walked to the door. They all hugged and kissed Lexi before they left, except for Aubrey, who was blissfully sleeping in Remi's arms. The McGuires were good people and like Sawyer, when you gained their trust, you had their loyalty.

Sawyer shut the door and armed the alarm. Lexi glanced at the clock and saw four am appear as she let out a yawn. Sawyer chuckled as he softly turned her shoulder and walked behind her up the stairs.

"Let's get you to bed..." he directed.

"You mean, let's get us to bed, right?" She turned and faced him. The desire in his eyes pooled and heat flushed through her body before he bent and tossed her over his shoulder in a fireman carry.

"I'm not too tired for that, sweetness," he growled before he tossed her onto the bed and kicked off his shoes.

"Thank goodness," she sighed, "I think ten years is long enough to wait, don't ya think?"

"Ten seconds is too long," he grumbled before he crawled up her body and seized her lips in a scorching kiss. The weight of his hard body was bliss. He kissed with such passion and fire that she was begging for more. He shifted and slowly left soft kisses down her nape and collarbone before he rose to capture her ear lobe between his teeth.

"You have no idea how much I've dreamt of this," he whispered seductively.

She moaned as his hands grazed the hem of her shirt. She quickly sat up and stripped off her shirt and pants. She grabbed Sawyer in a kiss and only broke to remove his shirt. She softly danced her fingertips over his firm abs and he hissed in pleasure at her touch.

"Pants. Off. Now." She demanded.

Sawyer stood and shucked his pants, "So bossy..." he grinned.

He gazed down at her from the end of her bed. He slowly roamed her body as if memorizing every inch of her skin into his memory. His eyes landed on the scars from the accident. She had multiple. A large one on her leg, where there were a titanium plate and screws. One on her stomach, where a shard of glass pierced her skin. And then the one on her face.

Lexi started to wonder if he was second-guessing everything now that he'd seen her body on full display. She made to cover herself with the blankets and he quickly grabbed them from her hands.

"Don't ever cover yourself for me, Lex?" he said seriously.

"I know the scars aren't pretty...."

"Stop," he interrupted as he moved up the bed laying kisses on her calves and pausing at the scar on her thigh before placing light kisses there.

"Every scar you have is a reminder that you're still here. And I've never seen anything more beautiful."

He used his fingers to slide her thong off her body before he continued his journey up her body. When his lips finally landed on hers, she was itching to have him inside her. She felt the large bulge in his briefs as it rubbed against her core. She ran her hands over his strong muscled back as he moved down to her breasts.

"Tell me what you want Lexi," he begged.

"You... I want you." she hissed.

"I know that darling. I meant how do you like it?"

"I'm not breakable if that's what you're asking," she countered.

At that moment he slid his tongue lightly over her waiting nipple. The lightest sensation but it set her on fire. He used his index and thumb to roll her other sensitive bud and pulled slightly.

"Oh, God..." she moaned.

He roughly sucked her nipple into his mouth and rolled it between his teeth causing her to arch into him. She'd been with men other than Sawyer before, but none of them felt like this. She yearned to touch him and make him moaned in delight.

"I want to taste you," he declared moving down her body, "Is this okay?" he asked.

Lexi was so entranced by her body's reaction to him that she didn't know if she answered. But she nodded and bit her lip. She'd never let men down there before. But she had a feeling Sawyer knew what he was doing.

He wiggled himself between her legs and used his strong calloused hands to push open her thighs. Without any warning, he ran his hot tongue from her entrance to her clit. Lexi's hips rose with the sensation.

"More..." was all she was able to gasp out in response.

With that, he spread her wet folds and using his tongue circled her clit. He rotated from hard pressure to the softest of grazes. He had her pleading for release as her hips rocked into him.

"God Lexi, you taste so sweet. I could do this all day," he said as he dove into her core again. This time he used his strong hands to penetrate her heat while he assaulted her clit. Lexi's hands flew to his hair as she felt her release build. It was as though she wasn't in control of her body because she wanted the release so desperately that she roughly grabbed him pushing him into her core.

"Baby, I'm going to come. Please Sawyer," she begged easing her grip briefly.

"Come for me, Lexi. I want to taste you as you come," he growled.

That was all the incentive she needed as he buried his face between her legs and rammed his fingers into her core fiercely. The orgasm rocked through her body as her legs gripped his head to her as she rode out the first wave. Once the spasms slowed, she anticipated that Sawyer would move on, but he didn't. He was hungry for her and he devoured her again. This time with more passion and vigour than before. He moaned against her core as he plundered her arousal. She felt a second wave erupt through her body and he pulled her clit into his mouth and sucked hard.

"Fuck...me," she screamed and collapsed back against the pillow.

"Your wish is my command," he said

slyly as he chucked his briefs and searched for a condom.

"I'm clean and I'm on the pill," she told him.

"I'm clean, but I've never…" he shook his head.

"Sawyer, if you don't get in me right this second I am going to lose my mind…"

He pulled her by her hips towards the end of the bed, placing her legs adjacent to his chest. He took his long hard cock and rubbed it against her core.

"You want this?" he teased.

She bit her lip and nodded. The next second he filled her to the core with a groan. Sawyer was a big man, in every way. She felt her walls clench around him slowly adjusting to his size. He filled her perfectly. It was as though they were two halves of a whole finally coming together.

"Fuck, you feel good," he hissed as his hips began to move slowly and she thrust upward to greet his movements. Sawyer pounded her over and over as beads of sweat rolled down his hard masculine chest. He shifted his hand to her clit and rubbed her sensitive bud eagerly. Light shattered behind her eyes as she screamed his name in ecstasy. She felt her walls clench around his member and heard the loud moan before his warm essence filled her to the rim.

Silently, he rose and grabbed a towel to clean up the mess they'd made. Then he lifted the sheets and tucked her inside before crawling in behind her. He kissed her shoulder sweetly.

"Go to sleep beautiful. I'm not going anywhere," he reassured.

She fell asleep in his warm embrace feeling assured that he would protect her from all her demons. At that moment, she found happiness and her heart felt whole for the first time in a decade.

Chapter 17

SAWYER

Sawyer woke as the sun hit his face from the bedroom window. He slowly opened his eyes and squinted while they adjusted to the light. He felt Lexi's warm body snuggled in tightly to his chest. She was still peacefully asleep so he took the opportunity to look at her. Her warm brown hair covered her face and he gently pushed it off her forehead. She let out a quiet sigh and his heart grew in his chest. He'd never spent the night with a woman. He never wanted to, but Lexi was different. She was the one who got away and now that he'd finally reconnected with her, he had no plans to let her go.

He ran his fingers lightly up the bare arm that was wrapped around his waist.

Lexi stirred before she looked up at him with a doe-eyed smile.

"Good morning," she mumbled cutely with a shy smile plastered on her face. She snuggled closer and pressed a kiss to his chest. Sawyer smiled and tipped her chin upward so he could capture her lips in a proper morning kiss.

"It is absolutely a good morning, sugar," Sawyer replied, as he broke the kiss and gazed into her iridescent green eyes. She shifted backwards and laid her small dainty hands on top of one of another before she placed her chin on her hands and stared up at him.

"So, Sheriff... What's the plan for today?" she asked.

"What do you have to do?" Sawyer asked as he tucked a runaway strain of hair behind her ear. She arched an eyebrow and a slow smile crept up her face.

"Well..." she said, "It's been a long time since I've had a man in my bed. Perhaps we can make the most of it before the McGuire's and the Scotts descend on our bliss."

"I like the way you think," he commented. He intertwined her hair around his hand and pulled her to him for a scorching kiss. She quickly jumped on top of him and straddled his hips. His hands moved to her hips. Their mouths danced in perfect harmony and the passion was fuelled by every whimper and moan she produced. She moved her kissing to his nape and she bit and sucked at his skin. She continued to move lower and plastered his strong chest with slow sensual kisses leaving fire in its path. She continued her descent down his body.

"I'm liking where this is going," Sawyer teased. Lexi caught his gaze as she reached the sensitive V under his abs. The anticipation was killing him and he'd longed to see Lexi eager and willing to wrap her hot plump lips around his shaft. He was just about to beg when his cell phone on the nightstand rang. Lexi froze and Sawyer cursed.

"Ignore it," he requested, but once the ringing ceased, his work cell started.

"Sheriff, I think you're needed," she

chuckled, as she moved up his body and wrapped herself in the sheet from the bed. Sawyer ran a frustrated hand down over his face as Lexi slid off the bed and strolled toward the bathroom.

"But what about what I need?" he groaned.

"Well, answer the call and if it's not urgent, you can join me in the shower," she winked and scurried into the bathroom. Sawyer heard the water run as he picked up his cell phone.

"This better be good Parker," he said, his tone dripped in irritation.

"W-Well sir, I think it's important," Parker replied.

"Well, go on with it," he commanded.

Parker cleared his throat, a sure sign that he was nervous. Parker was a good deputy and he was straight-laced, but sometimes he tried Sawyer's patience.

"Sir, a body has been found outside of City Hall."

With that, Sawyer sat up in bed and twisted his legs out of the bed. He padded his way to the bathroom while speaking with Parker.

"I'm on my way. Make sure the Coroner and the Deputies secure the scene. Do we have an ID yet?" He asked. Sawyer had only tackled one other murder investigation just after Aubrey came onto the scene and her ex hired a psycho to kill her. He ended up dead by her ex and Aubrey nearly lost her life in the process.

He was getting ahead of himself. He wasn't even sure it was a murder. For all, he knew old missus Harper could have dropped dead of natural caused.

"Not yet sure," Parker said.

"I'll be there in twenty," Sawyer said, but then he turned to see Lexi in the shower and his body said twenty wouldn't be long enough. "Make that thirty," he said before he hung up with Parker.

Sawyer joined Lexi in the tiled walk-in shower. Water ran over her back as she lifted her face towards the rain shower head. He walked in behind her and wrapped his arms around her waist and pulled her in to kiss her nape. She stretched her neck to the side and leaned into his body.

"What was that about?" she asked, her eyes closed as he moved down her shoulder.

"I have to go to the office in thirty minutes," he murmured against her skin.

"Oh, is it take your girlfriend to work day then?" she chuckled.

Girlfriend. Is that what she was now? He liked the sound of her being that to him. He wanted that, but they hadn't talked about what last night meant for them. Hell, he hadn't taken her on a proper date. Maybe with their long history, they'd skip past those awkward moments.

Sawyer's head lifted and he twirled her around to face him. Her arms instantly went to his shoulders and her hands intertwined behind his neck.

"Girlfriend?" he questioned raising one eyebrow inquisitively. Her eyes grew wide and he knew at that moment that she realized the slip of the tongue.

"Ah... Oh... Well, we haven't talked about what we are to each other after last night," she replied and he could see the insecurities on her face. She was unable to look him in the eye and her body tensed in his arms. Did she not know the impact she had on him? Or his feelings towards her after last night?

Sawyer gentled pushed her up against the tile wall. He grabbed her thighs and she gripped his hips securely. She moaned when her core came in contact with his arousal. He stole her lips in a passionate sensual kiss before he pulled back to look at her.

"Baby, I don't care what we call this as long as I get to do it every day," he growled, as she ground her hips against him.

"Mmmm, so we're dating, yeah?" She said sliding her lower lip between her teeth. He couldn't take it anymore and he shifted to slip deep inside her core. With a moan, she threw her head back in ecstasy.

"Yes, we're dating each other and only each other," he said, as he moved slowly inside her. She was wet and ready for him. He gripped her ass and pulled his cock out slowly before plunging it back into her tight heat.

"Fuck yes," she groaned.

He took his time pumping deep into her without caution. Every slide and pulse sent shivers of pleasure through his body. It was as though she was made for him. They fit together perfectly and the feelings he had when he made love to Lexi was different from any other experience. Sure, he'd fucked his fair share of ladies. But he'd never made love. He made love to Lexi and he wanted to do it as much as possible for the remainder of his lifetime.

Her gripped tighten on his hair and she yanked him to her before she demanded his lips. He savoured the taste of her and the feel of her tongue against his. She met his passion with eager sensuality.

"I need more Sawyer," she demanded in between kisses. He moved one hand in between their pounding bodies as he sought out the sensitive bud that he knew would send her over the edge. He rubbed her core without abandon and she screamed his name, her head tossed back in pure bliss as her pussy clenched around his hard cock.

"That's it, baby. Come for me…" he huffed, as he pulled out and thrust back in deep over and over again. Her body started to tremble with her orgasm and he pushed his forehead against the wall over her shoulder as he held on for her to come around him.

He felt the rush of heat build in his core and the tightness of his cock inside her throbbed with the need to release. Lexi's body continued to spasm as his pleasure met hers.

"Oh, God…I need you to come in me Sheriff," she whimpered.

The huskiness of her voice and the sex in her eyes were his undoing. His orgasm erupted inside her clenched and tight core. She arched into his thrusts as he rode out his pleasure. Once they'd both returned to solid ground, he hesitantly moved out of her, pressing a soft kiss to her lips as he did.

"We should shower like that every day," she smirked.

"Don't tempt me, woman," he re-torted. She chuckled and her smile brightened the entire world in Sawyer's eyes. They both showered and prepared for their day.

Sawyer was in the kitchen pouring them some coffee in to-go cups when she came downstairs. He handed her the coffee.

"Black?" She asked.

"Of course. I know what you like," he winked before pressing a kiss to her temple. "We need to get going. I'm going to drop you off with Finn and Remi while I take care of some work. I shouldn't be more than a couple of hours."

"Okay. It will be great to see Miss Martha and to properly catch up with Finn," she agreed while sipping her coffee and slipping on some tennis shoes. Her cowgirl cutoff jeans emphasized her long beautiful legs and her white tank top starred in a variety of his favourite fantasies. It was hard to think about anything else.

They jumped in the truck and made their way to the McGuire's ranch. Remi and the others would ensure that Lexi was safe while she was there. Finn's training put him at ease and Remi was just looking for people to beat when he has a reason.

"I'm just saying that if you have some obsession with Dolly Parton, that I wouldn't judge you," Lexi joked, as she stepped out of the truck and towards the farmhouse.

"Ain't nothing wrong with a bit of Dolly Parton, but that's not why her name is Jolene," he countered. Remi had often said that Jolene was a stupid name for his truck and sometimes he continued to use the name just to piss him off.

"Okay, so what's the reason?" she probed while ascending the farmhouse stairs.

Sawyer grabbed her around the waist and took her lips in a chaste kiss before he pulled back the screen door.

"A man needs to have some secrets darling. And if I told you, I'd have to kill you. So really it's for your protection..." he joked.

"Well, I'll be! If it isn't Lexi Scott!" Miss Martha ploughed towards Lexi and wrapped her arms around her in a tight embrace. Lexi returned the gesture. Lexi spent a lot of time around the ranch when they were growing up. She spent most of her summers with her Nana on the adjacent farm and her Nana and Miss Martha were the best of friends.

"Hello, Miss Martha. I'm so glad to see you," Lexi acknowledged. Miss Martha went in for another hug as she expressed her sympathies for Lexi's Nana.

Sawyer stood behind Lexi and watched the exchange. Normally Miss Martha dotted on him when he returned to the ranch.

"Hey... I thought I was your favourite!" he pouted sarcastically. Miss Martha finally pulled away from Lexi long enough to pat him on the cheek affectionately.

"Oh sweetheart, you know I don't have favourite," she announced before leaning in to whisper, "But if I did, it'd probably be the dog."

They chuckled together before moving into the kitchen where the entire McGuire Clan had come together for breakfast.

"Hey y'all," Sawyer said with a round of head nods and waves in his and Lexi's direction. A very hungover Aubrey stumbled her way downstairs and sat at the kitchen island. Her complexion was pale and she looked like an extra on the Walking Dead.

"Looks like someone should've laid off the vodka last night, huh?" Sawyer teased. He saw Remi smirk from the corner of his eye.

"Now, now brother, it's not like you haven't been hungover before..." Remi countered as he placed a full breakfast in front of Aubrey. She took one look at the food and ran for the bathroom to hurl. Sawyer threw his head back and laughed.

"Oh God, Remi you were right. It is a hell of a lot more fun when it's not you."

Miss Martha slapped Remi on the chest, "Boy, that is your wife. In sickness and in health until death do you part, remember?" She argued.

"Death might be coming sooner rather than later," Aubrey bellowed before they all erupted in laughter.

"Remi I need Lexi to stay here for the day. I got a call. Think you guys can handle her?" Sawyer asked. Lexi had already taken a seat next to Emma at the table and she was showing Lexi her Peppa Pig colouring book.

"Yeah shouldn't be any trouble. Everything alright?" Remi questioned.

"Yeah, everything is fine. I just don't want to traumatize her with a potential crime scene," he replied.

Remi nodded and with his promise not to lose sight of Lexi at all while she was there, Sawyer made his way to the dining room.

"Alright, y'all. I need to go. Duty calls," he announced. "You good here, Lex?"

She nodded, "Of course. Me and Emma are becoming fast friends." Emma's smile grew a thousand times.

"Okay, I'll see you later," he said before he leaned down and pressed a kiss to her lips.

"Ewwwww. Why does everyone do that?" Emma squealed causing a grin to spread across Lexi's face.

"Bobby Johnson kissed me on the playground once and it was gross," Emma continued.

"And when was this?" Remi asked as he entered the dining room.

"A while ago. But it never happened again. I think he learned his lesson," she explained. Remi crossed his arms and stared at the pint-sized little lady.

"What did you do to him?" he prompted.

Emma's head dropped in shame. "Emma..." Remi offered. Emma threw her hands up before admitting defeat.

"I made him eat dirt. But in fairness, he tried to kiss me first," she confessed.

Remi smiled at the little girl. She was going to be trouble when she got older, but they were all glad to see her defending herself in those scenarios.

"And that's my cue to leave," Sawyer chuckled before pressing another kiss on Lexi's lips. God, she tasted amazing. He was insatiable with her and he didn't believe he would ever have his fill of her.

He jumped in his truck and made his way to city hall. He pulled up and noticed the crime scene investigators on the scene and Parker waved him over.

"Sir," he addressed.

"This doesn't appear to be a natural death."

Sawyer quickly moved towards the body that was covered with a white sheet while the Coroner completed their assessment and the techs took photos and evidence. With gloves on, he removed the sheet to see a familiar face staring back at him. Even more alarming was the bloody note that had been sewn into the skin on her collar bone.

I've saved a special present for you, Lexi.

Every week that I don't get to see you, I'll kill another girl in this town.

Their blood is on your hands.

All I want… is you.

Make # 13 my last. - B

"Fuck" Sawyer cursed.

How the fuck was he going to tell Lexi about this. Brant couldn't have picked a better victim to get to her. Sawyer knew that if Lexi was given the option to meet with Brant to save the lives of other women that she would do it in a second. He wouldn't let her do that. With Brant in Silverton, Sawyer knew it was time to call in the big guys. They simply didn't have the resources to handle the kind of crazy Brant was serving up.

He'd call the FBI. But first, he had to figure out what he was going to tell the victim's family. The notification was one of the hardest parts of his job. Seeing the beautiful blue eyes staring back at him told him that he was out of his league here. It was his responsibility to protect Silverton and to protect her.

He sighed as he lifted the sheet back over her face, "It's Valerie Harper," he declared before he stood and made the call he didn't want to make.

Chapter 18

LEXI

"Go fish!" Emma squealed from her side of the coffee table. The little darling held her cards tight to her chest as she bellowed. She enjoyed saying "go fish" more than playing the actual game.

"You know, I should take you to Vegas with me so we could win some big money," Lexi joked.

So far the child had kicked her ass in every board and card game they thought of. Emma was without a doubt a charismatic and charming youngster. She was bright and confident, although there'd been times where Lexi saw her insecurities and the impact her childhood trauma had on her.

"Can I ask you a question, Miss Lexi?" Emma queried. She added curious to the growing list of characteristics for the child. If Lexi had a nickel for every time Emma asked "why?" she would never have to work ever again.

"Sure," Lexi shrugged. She could handle a question from the little bruiser.

Emma tilted her head to the side, kind of like a cute puppy when it heard a high pitch sound.

"Why do you have a scar on your face?"

Lexi's blood ran cold. She never grew comfortable with people asking that question. She always felt as though they were judging her based on the scar. But kids, they were different. They weren't born judgmental creatures. They don't arrive in the world with an inherited set of values and teachings. Children were taught how to hate and how to judge. And Emma, well she was just curious. Jordan was doing a wonderful job caring for Emma and her brother and she knew that the McGuire's fostered a positive environment for them. So, answering Emma's question wasn't as difficult as it could've been.

Lexi folded her cards down on the table before she looked at the little doll who sat across from her. Her face was so small and innocent and Lexi saw in her eyes that she meant to not harm. That was what ultimately decided for her that she would be honest with Emma about her trauma.

"Well, when I was in high school I had an accident," she said.

"What kind of accident?"

"I was hit by a car," she replied.

Emma squinted before she replied, "But, didn't you look before you crossed the street? Jordan always says that we need to do that to we don't get hurt."

Lexi smiled, "Jordan is very correct. You should always look before you cross the street and always have an adult with you," she agreed. "But unfortunately, the accident wasn't my fault. You see, the person driving the car that hit me had done something bad and against the law."

"They did?" Emma gasped and her blue eyes widened with concern.

"They did. You see, people aren't allowed to drink beer or wine and then drive their cars. But this person had and because of that she or he shouldn't have driven. I was just in the wrong place at the wrong time," Lexi tried to reassure her. It was a challenge, to be honest with the girl in a way that was easily understood by her little mind.

"Did Uncle Sawyer find them and put them in jail for being bad?" Emma asked.

Lexi hadn't heard anyone enter the house through the front door until she heard a voice from behind her.

"No, Uncle Sawyer was only a boy then too," Sawyer said, as he walked toward them and sat next to Lexi on the couch. "But because of what happened to Lexi, Uncle Sawyer promised himself that he would never let anyone he cared about get hurt like that again."

"So, that's why you put the bad guys in time out?" Emma asked. Sawyer's smile brightened the room as he gestured for Emma to go to him. She didn't flinch and rushed into his arms. He hugged her before settling her on his lap and pressing a kiss to her temple.

"Yeah munchkin, that's why I became a cop. And why I was a soldier," he said, as he turned his gaze toward Lexi.

He had said that her accident impacted him and changed his life path, but she didn't realize to what extent it impacted his whole life. It was a though he'd dedicated his life to making up for his past mistake. That night must've caused him so much pain. Only for her to push him away when he tried to help.

Her heart broke all over again and her eyes filled with unshed tears as she gazed into the deep emerald eyes of the strong man in front of her.

"Emma! Come get your lunch sweetheart," Miss Martha yelled out from the kitchen. Her southern drawl eased Lexi's heart and reminded her of the feeling of being home. Emma leaned into Sawyer and pressed a peck to his nose before she jumped off his lap and ran into the kitchen.

Once alone, silence cracked through the air. Sawyer's confession stood between them like a giant elephant in the room. How was she so blind to him all those years?

"Lexi..." he managed to say before her heart flipped inside her chest. It was at that moment that she realized how far gone she was. She was head over heels in love with him and she didn't think she ever stopped.

She moved quickly to close the distance between them. She felt she would explode if she didn't get to touch him. He was a cold drink of water in the middle of a draught. She gripped the back of his neck and collided with his lips. He let out a satisfied sigh as she curled into his hard body. His hands reflectively gripped her hips as she moved to straddle his lap. He broke free from her embraced with a cute chuckle.

"Not that I'm complaining Lex, but that's one hell of a greeting," he said, as she pressed a kiss to his neck. "It's the uniform isn't it?" he joked.

Lexi pulled back and gazed into the face of the man that she loved. She glanced at the clock and realized that it was only lunchtime and that Sawyer should still be on duty.

"Did you come back for lunch?

Maybe a bit of after delight?" she waggled her eyebrows comedically before leaning in to nuzzle his neck. Sawyer groaned and cursed.

"No, actually I needed to talk to you. And it would be a lot easier if you weren't the living embodiment of sex on a stick," he said, as his hands slowly caressed her back. On hearing his reply, Lexi immediately sat up.

"Something is wrong, isn't it?" she questioned. All traces of fun and happiness was stripped from her features. Sawyer took a deep breath before tucking a loose strand of hair behind her ear.

"Yeah, baby, something is wrong," he admitted, his eyes filled with sadness and Lexi knew that what he would say next would change everything for her.

"Tell me, Sawyer," she demanded. He grabbed both of her hands in his and interlaced their fingers.

"The body they found this morning..." he started, but Lexi already knew where he was going.

"It was Brant, wasn't it? He killed

someone..." she interrupted. Sawyer nodded and she saw grief and horror cross his beautiful face.

"Who?" she whispered. Her voice was soft and hesitant. She didn't want to know who Brant had killed. Whose life he had cut short because he couldn't get what he wanted. Sawyer was silent as Lexi's stare bored into him.

"Who!?" she yelled. He sighed and closed his forest green eyes.

"Valerie..." he whispered.

Lexi froze as she took the time to process the name he had just said. Valerie. Lexi's eyes filled with tears and despite her best efforts to prevent them from falling, they streamed down her face. Her hand flew to cover her mouth as a sob was pulled from her chest. Sawyer wrapped her in his arms and rubbed her back as she cried into his chest.

"Ssh, baby. I'm sorry. I'm so, so sorry," he murmured into her hair.

Lexi wasn't sure how long she spent curled in his embrace but once her body stopped shaking and her sobs no longer stole her voice, she sat up.

"He left a note?" she asked, but she already knew the answer. Brant was nothing, if not predictable. Sawyer nodded.

"I want to see it," she demanded, her voice strong and filled with rage.

"No," Sawyer replied. Simply no. There was no reason or explanation. Just no.

"Why not?" Lexi challenged, as she turned toward him on the couch. He wouldn't meet her eye and she knew why he wouldn't let her see the note.

"It was for me, wasn't it? He left the note for me."

"Lexi..." Sawyer started.

"No!" she said firmly, "He left that for me and I have every right to know why he decided to kill and how I can put a stop to this madness."

Sawyer stood and started to pace in front of her as they continued to argue about whether she should read the note or not. Their voices quickly heated and they were both frustrated and emotionally drained. Sawyer got to his knees in front of her as she sat and took her face in his strong calloused hands.

"I'm trying to protect you, Lex. It's not on you that this psycho murdered Val. It's not on you to fix this. You cannot hold yourself responsible for his actions," he said softly, as his thumbs reached across her cheeks to wipe away tears from her cheeks.

"He wants me, Sawyer. It should have been me. Now, Valerie's life is over and her parents..." she choked back a sob, "Oh Lord, her parents..."

"Look at me Lexi," Sawyer commanded, "it has taken me ten years to finally get you back where you belong. I will not let you leave me again. You belong here, with me and I won't let anyone or anything get in between that, you hear me?"

Lexi tilted her head before she simply nodded. He sighed and wrapped her in a hug. She could hear his heartbeat racing with fear. He pulled back and pressed a chaste kiss to her lips, lingering to savour the sweet tingle.

"You are not a price I'm ever going to pay, baby," he whispered against her lips.

"Okay…" she conceded. There was nothing she wouldn't give to Sawyer McGuire. "But I think you need to call the big guns to help with this. They would be interested to know if Brant has struck again."

"I've already called Agent Phillips. He is on his way and will be here in a couple of days. We just to do what we can until then. My priority is keeping you safe," Sawyer affirmed.

Sawyer stood and made his way to the door. As he did Jake appeared in the doorway, frazzled and frantic.

"Lexi! Lexi!" he looked around the ranch house until Lexi appeared before him. He grabbed her in a hug and planted kisses all over her face causing Lexi to erupt in giggles.

She saw Sawyer shrug as he tossed her a wink and tipped his cowboy hat before leaving the house. Lexi was finally set on her feet again and she had the chance to take in her brother's state. His shirt was untucked, his hair was a jungle and he looked as though he hadn't slept in days.

"Jack… what is wrong?" she asked cautiously.

"Jesus Lexi, I heard on the radio about the young female being found murdered on the steps of City Hall and my heart just dropped," he confessed before grabbing her in another hug.

"I'm fine Munchkin. It wasn't me. I'm here," she attempted to soothe him. She had never seen her brother so frazzled. Lexi was able to calm her brother when she mentioned Miss Martha's Pumpkin Pie.

Chapter 19

LEXI

Over the following two weeks, Brant continued to keep his promise and delivered two more young women to the morgue. Lexi's guilt over their deaths continued to play on her conscious. She couldn't help feeling responsible for their demise and the horrific nature of their deaths. Sawyer continued to drill into her that it was not her fault, but her internal struggle continued.

Sawyer and the McGuires were quickly becoming a constant in her ever-changing lifestyle. They were all committed to ensuring that the Scotts were taken care of while Brant was on the run. Lexi's parents had moved into the farmhouse with her and Jack to make it easier. It also prevented any further concern for their safety if they were all together.

Sawyer spent every night in her bed and their relationship continued to bloom despite the tension and conflict occurring around them. Every day he showered her with affection and assured her that she was where she belonged.

Lexi stirred from a night of deep sleep to find Sawyer transfixed on her face with a far off look gleaming in his eye. She smiled up at him through a yawn that had been working its way out.

"Good morning," she mumbled.

"Have I ever told you how adorable you are in the mornings?" he questioned.

Lexi sat up and allowed the sheets to fall across her waist revealing her naked chest. She walked her fingers up his chest before leaning down to plant a quick kiss on his lips.

"Mmm, nope I don't think you've told me that before, but cute isn't really what I'm feeling right now..." she countered as she slowly moved to straddle his hips. His hands quickly roamed up her arms and lightly caressed her breasts.

"No? So what are you feeling then?" he asked with a sexy hooded light in his eye. She bit her lip as she slowly pulled her core across his length and he growled.

"Sexy? Hot? Tempting? Those are all perfectly acceptable," she smiled as she continued to rub her core against his. His hands grasped her as and he pulled her roughly against him causing a moan to slip from her throat.

"You're insatiable," he mumbled against her skin as he raised his mouth to nip at her exposed breast. He licked softly around her nipple before sucking it hard into his hot waiting mouth. He used his tongue to slowly flick and sucked the sensitive bud. Lexi was whimpering in need by the time he was done and he pressed kisses lower and shifted his body under hers so that his face was between her thighs and in contact with her core.

"Grab the headboard," he commanded. When Lexi didn't do as she was told he offered a slap across her ass. The tingle of his handprint stung her skin but the pleasure jolted her out of her daze. She quickly grabbed the wooden headboard as Sawyer pushed open her thighs farther. Using his fingers he parted her folds before thrusting a finger deep inside.

"Fuck baby, you're already wet for me," he groaned before he swiped his tongue from her entrance to her clit. He spread her folds and softly circled her sensitive bud while thrusting his fingers into her core. He moaned with every lick of his tongue and his pleasure intensified her desire. Her body became his and only his and when she locked eyes with him as he devoured her, her orgasm built to an ultimate high.

"Fuck…" she hissed. Sawyer knew her climax was building and he picked up the speed and vigorously sucked on her clit while curling his fingers to stroke that sweet spot her knew would make her crumble. Her hips gyrated over his face of their own free will and her legs began to tremble from pleasure.

"Baby come for me. You taste so good. Come for me," he groaned as she continued to move over his face. God, he was amazing. The heat built inside her and she felt the rush of warmth escape her core as she gripped the headboard.

"Yes, Sawyer don't stop. Fuck," she moaned as she came roughly as he sucked her clit and pummelled her core. Once she had ridden out her tremors of pleasure, she collapsed on the bed next to Sawyer.

"You're amazing," she panted. He chuckled and made to get out of bed. She grabbed him by the hips and pushed him back.

"Where do you think you're going Sheriff?" she asked, straddling him and holding his hands over his head.

"Well, Ms Scott... I was going to get ready for my day," he grinned.

"Tsk tsk, I'm not done with you yet," she said, as she lined his pulsing erection against her entrance. In one swift movement, she slid herself down his length.

"Jesus," Sawyer hissed, as Lexi released his hands so he could grasp her hips. He filled her so well and she'd never had that feeling with anyone else. They were two parts of one whole and when he was with her, she felt her heart overflow with love.

Lexi began to push and pull herself up and down his shaft and moaned as he rose to meet her thrusts. She loved this man and she wanted to show him how much she loved him. She picked up the pace and Sawyer grabbed her nape and pulled her towards him. He intertwined his hands in her hair and took control of her mouth in a scorching kiss. Lexi's body began to climax and she clenched around his cock hard. Her legs began to shake and Sawyer quickly flipped the position so that she was bent forward with him behind her. He wasted no time ploughing into her core and gripping her hips so hard she was certain there would be bruises later.

Her back arched as her climax erupted and her pussy tugged on his cock in a tight hold. Sawyer continued to fuck her as their two bodies slapped together in ecstasy. All that could be heard in the room was their panting and the sound of flesh pounding into flesh.

"I'm gonna come, Lex," Sawyer groaned.

"Yes, baby," she screamed as Sawyer plundered into her hard and deep until a shutter wrecked his body and the warmth of his essence filled her core. They both collapsed onto the bed and he pulled her to him where he was and demanded a sweet slow kiss.

"You're amazing," he praised.

"And lucky for you, we get to do that again in twelve hours," she said before she hauled the sheet around her body. She rose and quickly hopped in the shower before coming out dressed for her day. She leaned on the door frame as she watched Sawyer fiddle with his holster and clipped on his badge. He looked over his shoulder and caught her staring at   him.

"Something wrong, darling?" he asked.

"No, I'm just reminded every day how risky your job is and that there is a chance that you'll walk out that door and won't come back," she admitted.

Sawyer strode across the room and

wrapped his arms around Lexi before he captured her lips in a sweet kiss.

"I'll always come home for you Lexi," he whispered.

"Sawyer…" she mumbled.

"Yes, Lex?" he replied.

"I have a confession to make," she continued.

He arched an eyebrow on his absurdly handsome face, "Do I have to get the handcuffs? 'Cause I'm down with that if you are."

She laughed and bit her lip as she pondered how to approach what she wanted to tell him. She closed her eyes and let out a long sigh. She pushed her gaze to her hands where she fiddled with her nails nervously. She'd never told anyone how she felt and she was a little worried that the man before her had the power to destroy her if he wanted.

"I'm in love with you…" she softly confessed, hoping that he didn't hear her. But she suspected he did as his body tensed and his heart began to race. He stared at her for a long time, or what felt like a long time for her before the buzz of his work cell phone sounded in his pocket.

Lexi knew that if he was going to reciprocate the feelings that he would have done so in that long awkward bit of time. She tried desperately not to let the hurt show on her face but she failed.

"Lexi..." he started, as his phone continued to buzz and he sighed before dropping his head. Lexi quickly shifted out of his grasp.

"I'll see you later," she said brightly. She was a "fake it 'till you make it" kind of girl and she didn't want him to know how much he hesitancy impacted her. She quickly shoved on her boots and made her way to the horse barn where Jack was helping in the care of a mare who gave birth the night before.

Jack was bent down in the stall with Rita as she cleaned and licked her little guy. He was still wobbly on his feet but was quickly getting used to the new world he came into less than twenty-four hours before.

"He seems to be doing well. How's

Mama doing?" she asked from the door.

Jack turned and smiled. He loved everything about ranching, even the hard stuff. The vet had been able to help deliver the mare but Jack would have been more than prepared to do it himself.

"She's doing well, ain't she Jack?" a strong familiar voice boomed through the barn. Lexi turned and came face to face with Finn.

"Hey Finn, I'm surprised to see you here," she greeted him with a kiss on the cheek.

"Hey Lex, we offered to help out Jack here for a bit since Remi and the hands seem to have things under control over there," he said.

"We?" she asked.

"Yeah, Leo is with me. Leo, don't be rude, say hello to Ms Scott," Finn prompted.

Leo popped his head out from behind Finn's broad shoulders. He was so tiny that he could easily hide behind the hulk of a man Finn had turned into.

"Hi Miss Scott," he greeted shyly.

"How's it going, Leo? Are you keeping yourself out of trouble as I told you to?" she asked firmly. Leo dropped his head as a blush flourished across his boyish face.

"Yes, ma'am…"

"Good. I don't want to have to represent you in court again, right?"

"No, ma'am…"

Lexi moved forward and hugged the boy with a smile, "I'm sure if you're learning from Finn that you'll turn out to be a fine man. Well-deserving of the name McGuire."

She mussed up his hair before she went to the barn door to check if Sawyer had left the farm yet. His squad car was gone and she breathed a sigh of relief.

"Something troubling ya, Lex?" Finn asked, startling her. She jumped at the sound of his voice. Turning she realized that Finn had followed her to the barn door.

"No, just checking on something," she said with ease.

"What's going on, sugar? I know you better than you know yourself remember. So I can tell when something is bothering you," he challenged. And of course, he was right. Finn was one of her best friends when he was around. Her mother always thought that they would make a good couple and tried to put them together as much as possible. But there had never been a connection with Finn in that way. There was no spark. No desire. No passion.

Their relationship bloomed into a great friendship and one that helped her through her heartbreak and helped Finn through the loss of both his parents.

She let out a big sigh, "Yeah a lot is bothering me. So much that I don't know where to even start. Everything seems out of my control and I feel like I am swimming upstream with no end in sight."

"Does this have something to do with my brother or with the raging serial killer?"

Lexi let out a sad laugh as the ridiculousness of that sentence. "You know if you had told me two months ago that I would be living on this ranch, in some sort of a relationship with Sawyer McGuire and had a serial killer on the hunt for me, I would have told you that you were crazy," she acknowledged.

"I can see that. How about we go get some breakfast? Dolly still has the best apple pie and I know you love something sweet in the morning," he said. She didn't need to be persuaded when it came to Dolly's apple pie. The woman sure knew how to cook and Lexi would pay to see her and Miss Martha in a cook-off. It would be like Martha Stewart and Gordon Ramsey duking it out in the kitchen.

"Sure, I could use some time away from this place, honestly," he confessed.

Finn smiled before he turned and told Jack to watch Leo while he took Lexi out for something to eat. Of course, Jack had a mile-high list of things he wanted to be ordered for himself. They walked toward Finn's truck and when Lexi saw it, she stopped dead in her tracks.

Of course, Finn couldn't just get a regular truck. Nope... He had to have it cranked up and decked out with a bunch of crap. Sawyer would say it was classic overcompensation and would hint that he had a small dick. Finn would easily pink Sawyer to the ground until he called mercy and that would be the end of it.

"How the hell do you supposed my ass is getting up in that? I need a God damn ladder!" she barked.

Finn chuckled and he moved to the passenger side door, "I'll give ya a boost, Lex."

"You're gonna have to. Jesus, I can't imagine you'd ever get a girl home in that thing. If she slipped trying to get in she would fall a good twenty feet," she poked.

She was being sarcastic and he knew it. She also knew that Finn had no problems getting female company and that any woman in the county would climb Everest just for a roll in the hay with him. His little truck was no match for a determined horny woman.

Once Lexi was situated in the truck, they began the drive into town. Silverton wasn't a large place, but it was big enough that someone could get lost in a crowd. Locals knew everything there was to know about the other and if they didn't know, they made it up. Gossip was the biggest trigger for relationship deterioration.

They pulled into Dolly's Dinner and took a booth by the window. The bright red booths with the black and white checkered floor reminded her of her youth. Countless milkshakes and plates of pie were shared there. She'd spent a lot of time remembering her past, especially after Valerie's death. She regretted not talking to her that day in the bakery. She should've mended the bridge and reconnected with her. But her pride prevented her from doing that and now Valerie was gone and she would never hear what she needed to say.

"So, what's bothering you?" Finn asked, ripping her out of her haze of memories.

A young girl with bright pink hair trotted over to the table. She had a piercing in her eyebrow, nose and lip. If the girl had any more holes in her face, Lexi could use her as a pasta strainer. She appeared to have no desire for her job and would probably have a better time watching paint dry.

"What can I getcha?" she asked.

"Two apple pies and chocolate milkshakes and we'll also have this to go," Finn replied, gesturing for her to take the note where Jack had written down his grocery list.

"Sure thing,"

Once she was gone to take care of the next table, well, maybe "take care" wasn't the right adjective. But once she left, Finn's attention shifted fully on her. He just stared at her and he knew it made her squirm. She hated when people stared her down and Finn had mastered the stare by eighth grade.

"So, two problems," she started.

"I assume one is the serial killer and the other is my dumbass brother," he answered.

"Correct. Now, the serial killer I can figure out. I know what he wants and what he will keep doing if he doesn't get it or get caught," she paused and Finn nodded for her to continue. "But Sawyer, I have no idea what I'm doing. I think I may have fucked it all up, Finn."

The punk waitress came back with their orders and quickly flew away. Finn took a bite of the pie and groaned. It was a common occurrence for people to make noise when they tasted Dolly's cooking.

"What did you do to fuck up? Honestly, I had money on Sawyer fucking it up before you."

Lexi put her face in her palms and groaned. She hated that she was second-guessing her feelings. She was always the one who knew what she was doing and had planned out her life in advance. Since Nana threw a wrench into her plans two months ago, she'd been feeling out of control.

"I told him I loved him and he said nothing," she confessed.

Finn narrowed his eyes and his brows pinched together. He looked constipated, which meant he was working out something in his head.

"He never said it back?"

"Nope," she said, pulling the fork from her mouth as she talked.

"Well, fuck, darling that's about him, not about you," he said reaching over to grasp her hand as a sign of comfort. "not to mention, if he doesn't know it he is a dumbass. But that boy has been in love with you since Kindergarten. Mama even said so."

"We've changed a lot since preschool Finn. We have lived and there have been complications. Jesus, I don't even know how long I'll be around," she noted.

Finn pointed his fork as her, "Now, that's enough of that. This place will always be your home, Lexi. I think you need to talk with Sawyer. Or I can talk to him for you," he probed.

"No!" Lexi shouted, drawing the attention of other patrons in the diner.

"No," she said softly, "I need to figure this out on my own."

The bell above Dolly's door rung and in walked a man in a suit and aviator sunglasses. She could spot a FED anywhere and that man was a walking talking recruitment ad. He looked around briefly before his eyes landed on her.

"I think we have company," she told Finn, as the man started walking toward them.

"Miss Scott?" he asked, as he took off his aviators.

"Yes, and you are?" Lexi countered.

"Agent Phillips from the FBI. I'm sorry we are a bit behind, but we are here now," Phillips offered.

"I'd like to take your statement for the FBI file and was wondering if you would be free to do that with me?"

"Sure," she looked at Finn and he waved her off after he checked the agent's credentials.

"Don't worry about me. You go on with Agent Phillips and I'll let lover boy know where you are," Finn said.

Lexi pressed a kiss to his cheek before grabbing her purse and exiting Dolly's with Agent Phillips. She jumped into his black SUV with tinted windows. The doors locked automatically as he began to drive, but she realized that she wasn't headed back to the farmhouse. They were headed out of the city.

"Agent Phillips, the ranch house is back there," she said, as they passed the turnoff for her home.

"I know," Phillips replied, "we're not going there. I have someone who desperately wants to meet you, Miss Scott."

Lexi's pulse jumped instantly and her heart began to beat rapidly in her chest. She made to unlock the door only to find that Phillips had disengaged the locks. She was trapped and no one would look for her for hours as they'd think she was safe with an agent.

The next thing that happened, happened quickly. Phillips pulled a syringe from the console, put the cover in his mouth to get the needle out.

"What the fuck is that!?" she bellowed, but not before he jabbed her in the thigh with the unknown substance.

"I'm just tired of hearing you talk," he said. And this was the last thing she heard before everything went black and the silence overwhelmed her.

Chapter 20

SAWYER

He was an idiot.

If his father could talk to him now, he would agree.

He knew how he felt about Lexi. Jesus, he'd always known that he loved her. From the first time she pushed Bobby James on the playground in Kindergarten, he knew she was the one for him. It explained why he never felt the urge to settle down with anyone before. He'd been waiting for Lexi.

He. Was. An. Idiot.

Sawyer banged his head on his steering wheel once he parked in front of the Sheriff's office. He went through his conversation with Lexi over and over in his head. He should have just told her he felt the same way, but the words wouldn't leave his mouth. Sawyer wanted to tell her more than anything else, but he questioned whether her feelings were real. All the hype about a potential serial killer and needing to stay on the ranch was off the charts.

If Lexi was faced with staying in Silverton with him or returning to her fancy life in New York, what would she choose? He was playing it safe. He knew she could leave at any time without a second glance. She'd done it before and it broke his heart into a million pieces. He wasn't sure he could put his heart of the line if she wasn't as committed as he was. One thing was clear to him, they needed to have a serious conversation about where the relationship was and where it was going.

Sawyer heard a gentle rap on the driver side window of his patrol car. He jumped out of his daze and turned to look at Parker. He really would rather stay in bed all day with Lexi, talking out the future. But, he was needed. Sawyer took a deep breath and opened his door, exiting to greet Parker.

"Morning Deputy," he greeted.

"Morning Sheriff," Parker replied as he turned to follow behind Sawyer.

"How was everything overnight?" Sawyer questioned. He made a point to check in on his Deputies and he didn't expect them to do anything he wouldn't do himself.

"Everything was quiet from what Rogers reported," Parker answered.

Sawyer entered the blissfully air-conditioned building, greeting the receptionist and other staff as he made his way back to his office. He got the full report from Parker and got busy doing paperwork and a conference call with the Mayor. Chase wasn't his favourite person since he left his sister heartbroken and jaded, but he was one hell of a mayor and he was keeping a close eye on the issue of Brant.

He was about to take a lunch break when a knock came on his door. He told whoever to enter and in walked his brother, Finn and his best friend, Brett. Both took the seats in front of his desk with serious expressions shadowing their faces. Sawyer's radar immediately went on high alert.

"Hey, what are you guys doing here?" he asked surprised.

Finn crossed his arms over his very large and abnormal chest before tossing a fierce scowl his way.

"You're a jackass," he mumbled.

"You're gonna need to narrow it down a bit for me," Sawyer admitted, putting his head in his hands with a sigh. He could think of several reasons he was a jackass and the list was growing exponentially.

"I believe what my beefed up friend here is trying to say is..." Brett said calmly.

"You're a class A jackass," Finn finished. Brett tossed his head back and prayed to someone for patience.

"Okay," Sawyer sighed, "me being a jackass seems to be a well-established fact. But, can you tell me why I am one today?"

"Do you love Lexi?" Finn barked out the question. The question caught Sawyer off guard. Why the fuck would his brother be asking whether he loved Lexi? Sawyer's jaw dropped in shock.

"How is my relationship with Lexi any of your business?" Sawyer countered, his fists clenched at his side.   He'd often felt jealous of the relationship Finn had with Lexi. Even after the accident, Lexi kept in touch with Finn and their parents always commented on how great of a couple they would be. Finn's face turned a deep shade of red and Sawyer could tell that he was trying hard to keep his temper in check. Finn never did have much patience when it came to Sawyer. Sawyer thought it was his job growing up to torment him. In fairness, Remi tormented him and he felt it was his right as the older brother to pass it along. He was starting to think that maybe he should've been nicer to the pissed off brute of a man sitting in his office.

"Anything that has to do with Lexi is my business, Sawyer," Finn gritted from between clenched teeth.

Sawyer's blood started to boil and his anger unleashed. Why was his brother so fucking interested in his relationship with Lexi? Sawyer's voice raised and he pushed back his office chair causing the scrapes to echo through the office.

"What the fuck does that mean?" he

bellowed. Finn stood to face Sawyer who was essentially foaming at the mouth.

"Fellas, fellas, can't we just keep the macho bullshit at the door for a second please?" Brett retorted while wiggling himself in between the two brothers.

"No! I want to know why my brother is asking about my girlfriend. Why Finn? Do you love Lexi? Is that it?" Sawyer yelled and he felt the vein in his forehead throb. His heartfelt as though it was going to bust out of his chest. He didn't want to kick his brother's ass. But he would.

"Of course I love Lexi! She's my best friend!" Finn screamed, "And I'm tired of picking up the pieces after you've blown up her heart again."

"What the fuck are you talking about?" Sawyer asked exasperated with the conversation.

"You!" Finn pointed his stupid finger in his chest forcefully, "Do you love her? It's a pretty simple question, Sawyer!"

Brett sat back in his chair and gave up hope that he could calm down the situation. It wasn't his first time mediating conflict between Sawyer and his siblings. If he could deal with Sara throwing down in the grocery store, then he could master the McGuires.

Sawyer ran his hands through his hair and pulled on the ends in frustration. He paced the small space behind his desk.

"OF COURSE I LOVE HER!" he screamed, certain the whole office had stopped what they were doing to listen to their not so quiet conversation.

"THEN WHY DIDN'T YOU TELL HER THAT?" Finn yelled back.

Now he understood. Finn was privy to his fuck up from that morning. He and Lexi were close and sure, Sawyer had been jealous of their relationship, but Finn has always treated her like the third sister they never had. Feeling defeated, he tossed his head back and sighed before he slumped back in his chair.

"I don't know..." he muttered.

Finn must have recognized that Sawyer had lost his will to fight with him anymore because he came around his desk and sat on the corner. Finn clasped his shoulder as Sawyer ran his fingers over his brow.

"Brother, I love you and I love her. The two of you together is amazing," he said gently. "When I got home, I saw how Aubrey and Remi look at each other and the change in him is so bone-deep its fucking nerve-racking. The man is in love and he is walking on god damn sunshine."

Sawyer let out a small chuckle, "You weren't here when they hated each other. I got in between far too many weird eye fucking sessions."

"I bet. But I see how you look at Lexi and how she looks at you. And Sawyer, it's the same way that stupid asshat looks at Aubrey. You need to own it and she needs to know," Finn continued.

"I know, Jesus, I know that. But... Fuck, what if she wakes up one day and decides she wants to go back to her fancy life back in New York? What if I'm not enough for her?" Sawyer plopped his head on the desk, "Fuck I sound like a woman."

"I was just about to ask if you needed tampons and some chocolate for this little meltdown," Brett piped in.

"Dude, you haven't lived with Jordan and Daisy during the formative years. Periods are no joke, my friend. Something you will find out yourself in about eight years" Finn challenged.

"And you need to give yourself more credit!" Finn argued turning his full attention back on Sawyer.

"You talked to Lex?" he asked.

"I took her for breakfast this morning. I could tell something was wrong."

Sawyer leaned back and let out a groan, "I don't know why I keep fucking it royally with her. How was she this morning?"

"Honestly?" Finn asked.

"Honestly. No bull."

"She was hurt. Questioning everything. But I never got to finish my conversation with her because Phillips came to get her statement," Finn said.

Phillips? Agent Phillips wasn't due until tomorrow and he had called to check in just that morning to let them know his flight had been delayed due to a storm in the Midwest. Why did he go to Lexi before checking in with him? His radar started to flicker and a storm started to brew in his stomach.

"Wait… Agent Phillips?" Sawyer questioned.

"Yeah, middle-aged suit with aviators and a 'don't piss me off 'face," Finn added.

Okay, that sounded accurate. Maybe he was confusing his days again. It wouldn't be the first time that happened. God knew he needed a vacation.

"Lexi is worth the risk, Sawyer," Brett said, returning the conversation to the topic at hand. "I know you don't want to get hurt and it's hard losing someone you love," he sighed and Sawyer knew he was thinking of Lucy. "But there isn't a day that goes by that I don't smile over the happy times I had with Lucy, even if in the end there wasn't forever," Brett continued.

"Daddy! Look!" a squeal was heard before a little ball of energy flew in through the door. Sara ran directly into her father's arms and showed him the sucker Parker had given her.

"Princess, did you thank Deputy Parker for the candy?" Brett prompted.

"MMMhmmmm" she murmured around the candy stuffed in her mouth. Brett leaned in and kissed her forehead before he turned to Sawyer.

"Despite the hurt, I got the greatest parts of her with me in this one and I don't regret taking the risk and never will," Brett said, his eyes filled with unshed tears as they often did when they spoke of Lucy. Brett never got back out there after Lucy and told Sawyer that he already had a lady in his life who consumed his entire life. And she deserved everything he had to give.

"You're right," Sawyer admitted.

"Daddy's always wright uncle Sawyer," Sara said seriously.

God, she was so much like her mother that it almost hurt his heart.

"Yeah he is kiddo," Sawyer agreed.

"So, how are you gonna fix this mess?" Finn asked from his perch on Sawyer's desk.

"I guess some grovelling and some major wooing," he announced.

"That's a start," Finn smiled down at him.

"Uncle Sawyer, will you come to lunch with us? Daddy said I could have ice cream if I was good in the grocery store," Sara perked up and her enthusiasm could be heard all the way to Dolly's Diner.

"And were you good at the grocery store?" he asked.

Sara shrugged as her father shook his head behind her, "Good enough," she commented.

"Sounds about right. Sure thing kiddo, but can you help after lunch pick out something for a girl?" Sawyer asked.

He tried hard to include Sara as much in his life as possible. Brett was doing a great job acting as both parents, but everyone needed help sometimes. And he wanted Sara to know that he would be there through everything. He liked the idea of being the "cool uncle".

Sara's face brightened and she clapped her hands together with excitement, "Yes!"

Sawyer popped up from his chair and

walked to the bubbly princess. She eagerly jumped from her father's lap and put her small delicate hand in his. His heart swelled every time she did that.

Sawyer spent the rest of the after-noon with Emma and Brett. He knew that Lexi was with the FBI and didn't worry about her. He also wasn't concerned when she didn't call or text him throughout the day. She was pissed and hurt and probably need some time to process everything.

After lunch, he took Emma to the local florist and got some fresh cut flowers. He went to the grocery store and picked up some items to make dinner that evening. Emma even helped him set up a table for two out by the lake. She helped him pick out a dress jacket for the evening and was a very opinionated little one.

"That one doesn't look nice," she barked, as Sawyer hauled on a navy blazer. She sat with her father on his bed, her little legs swinging from the edge. He put on another cowboy jacket that he owned in the mid-90s. Brown leather with fringes that lined the arms. Sara's face screwed up as though she smelt some foul odour. Sawyer spread his arms and twirled.

"It makes you look like a funny bird," she chuckled and Brett laughed from beside her.

"Woman, you're gonna be hard to please when you get older," Sawyer said.

After a long debate about why he couldn't wear a feather boa and tiara to the tea party, Brett and Emma went on their way. Sawyer sat patiently in the living room while he waited for Lexi to return to the farmhouse with Phillips.

"Me-owwwww," a catcall rung out, as Remi and Aubrey strolled through the door.

"Where are you off to done up like a very fine stick of chewing gum?" Aubrey asked as she took in his fancy appearance.

"Did you just call my brother fine?" Remi asked from behind her.

"Sure did!" Aubrey exclaimed. She knew how much Remi hated feeling like her attention was anywhere but on him. A sharp slap rang through the air and Aubrey yelped before Remi picked her up and tossed her over his shoulder.

"Put me down you maniac!" she screamed between laughter.

"Nope, we're going home and I'm going to remind you why you only compliment me!" Remi said a smile prominent on his face. "Where ever your ass is going brother, I hope you're not overdressed."

Sawyer shook his head before moving into the kitchen to grab a beer. He needed to settle his nerves. He sat at the island until it was approaching six pm. Surely gathering Lexi's statement didn't take Phillips that long.

He was just about to whip out his phone and call her when a knock sounded on the door. When he opened the door he found a blond mid-thirties man in a suit and tie. He had a badge clipped to his waist and carried a duffle bag.

"Can I help you?" Sawyer asked.

"Sheriff?" the man questioned.

"Yes," Sawyer dragged out the words. His hesitancy was clear.

"I'm Agent Phillips. We talked on the phone," he announced.

Sawyer blinked slowly as he tried to process what he heard. Lexi was with Agent Phillips and had been for most of the day. But the man on the stoop had a badge and brought a duffle bag as Sawyer told him there would be accommodations on the ranch. Sawyer did not doubt that the man who stood before him was FBI.

If Lexi wasn't with Agent Phillips, who was she with? And why did he suddenly feel like he was having a heart attack?

Chapter 21

LEXI

Lexi stirred with an urge to vomit. She was nauseous and still a bit dizzy. Her eyelids felt heavy and she struggled to get them open. She was going to kill Brant if she ever saw him again. With great difficulty, she was able to lift one eyelid to take in her surroundings.

Where the fuck was she?

She took a minute to orient herself and thought for sure that she was dreaming. And not a nice dream, you know like unicorns and rainbows. This was a fucking nightmare. She lifted her left hand to rub her eyes and felt the sting of metal on her wrists. She quickly startled into reality and looked at herself.

She was locked to a bed and she could feel the sting from where she had been trying to get her hand free. The skin surrounding the chain was red and fresh blood trickled down her arm. Her right hand was free of any kind of bondage, so she twisted herself and sat up on the side of the bed. Her head was fuzzy and she squinted to see.

"What the fuck?".

The floor and walls were concrete and she sat on a small double bed that had a metal bed frame. The chain attached to her left wrist was bolted into the wall and despite her attempts to break free, she was unsuccessful. There was a small desk to the side that held a single desk lamp which lit the room. In the corner, there was a small bucket and Lexi forced herself not to think about the purpose of the bucket. Lexi realized that it wasn't a nightmare. That she was indeed being held captive by Brant and that she had no clue as to where she was. She collapsed onto the floor and pulled her knees to her chest as sobs wracked through her.

She'd just realized that she loved a man and was willing to give everything up to be with him. Sawyer would know that she was gone and he would move heaven and hell to find her. She knew he would. How long had she been gone? Surely long enough that he would be worried. She rested her head on her arms as she curled into herself.

The sound of metal opening caused her to jump. She stood and pushed herself into the wall and sought anything in the room that could be a weapon. Of course, there was nothing. Brant wasn't stupid.

"Hello, pet," Brant cooed from his spot by the door.   He looked casual and relaxed wearing a pair of jeans and a black t-shirt. The mere sound of his voice caused chills to course through her body. She never thought she would be in a position where she would be at his mercy.

Brant slid himself closer to her and Lexi struggled not to flinch at his proximity to her. She felt his breath on her face and she forced herself not to shake in his presence. He raised his hand and caressed her cheek and Lexi fought back the urge to vomit, again.

"You're more beautiful now than

you were the last time I saw you," he whispered.

"You're a sick son of a bitch Brant," Lexi hissed.

He leaned into her and whispered into her ear. His breath was warm on her neck as he slowed his movements. He knew she was shaking and scared. The fucker thrived on it. He needed to create fear in his victims and Lexi wasn't about to show him that she was scared.

"Oh my pet," he whispered, "I've been waiting a long time for you, and I'm going to savour every moment we get together. But for right now, I have another matter to take care of. I believe her name is Carly. You know how I like to keep to a schedule, Lexi."

Lexi's heart dropped at the thought that Brant had another victim wherever they were. Another girl who was being tortured or worse. She also knew that Carly was only eighteen and was just a child.

"She's just a child. Let her go and do what you want with me," Lexi hissed, her gaze rose to meet his stare.

Brant was an attractive man by all accounts. He always presented as a well put together man with his wrinkle-free clothing and always freshly shaven. He was taller than Lexi at six feet, medium build with bland facial features and nothing that would cause him to stand out. He was average in every sense of the word. But inside his mind, he was sick.

Lexi thought about that for a second. She knew him better than anyone. She knew more about Brant than any of his victims and she could use that to her advantage. She knew what ticked him off and what he wanted to hear from his mother.

"Brant, she's someone's baby. Like you were at one time. Do you remember being eighteen?" Lexi asked calmly. She had to outsmart him that was the only way she would get the upper hand. He would easily overpower her physically.

Brant just stared into her eyes and she refused to look away.

"When you were her age, what did you want?" Lexi asked.

Brant's left eye twitched and she

knew that she was getting inside his head. He shifted and pushed himself against her. The weight of his body flushed up against her before he pushed back with a smirk on his face.

"What I wanted at her age is irrelevant Ms Scott. This is what I got," he growled and rose his shirt to show the scars on his torso. "We don't get what we want and neither will she. She's said she wants to die, but I won't let her. I'll decide what she wants now, Ms Scott. And once I'm done, I'll be back for you," he hissed before he turned on his heel and exited the room.

Lexi fell to the floor again and her nausea overwhelmed her and she tossed her cookies. She laid on the bed as her tears fell from her eyes onto the dirty mattress. It was then that she heard the screams of Carly and her pleas. Lexi tried to run to the door but was held back by her chains. She started to scream and hit things before she collapsed on the floor with her hands over her ears trying to not hear the sounds of death that engulfed the room.

SAWYER

Sawyer stared shell shocked at the man who stood on his porch. Every hair on his body stood at attention and his heart felt like it was about to beat out of his chest.

"Sheriff, you don't look too good," Phillips said pushing through the door as Sawyer stumbled backwards. Phillips grabbed him and helped him to the sofa.

"If you're Phillips, who the fuck has had Lexi all day?" Sawyer panted out. Sawyer saw the moment Phillips made the connections and the man's face lost all its colour.

The back door slammed shut as Finn and Jack made their way to the kitchen, completely oblivious to the panic occurring in the living room. Finn snuck around the corner to stumble upon the scene unfolding and his steps faltered.

"Sawyer..." he said hesitantly. Finn knew his brother and he would be able to tell just with a glance that something was off.

"What's happening?" Jack asked as he moved to stand next to Finn with a beer in his hand.

"He has Lexi," Sawyer breath out. He sat unable to move or speak as the realization dawned on Jack.

"What the fuck do you mean Sawyer? Who has Lexi?" Jack gritted through clenched teeth.

"Brant," Phillips answered.

"And you are?" Finn questioned.

"Agent Phillips with the FBI," Phillips replied and Finn's face dropped.

"No, Phillips took Lexi this morning for her statement. I was there when he went to the diner to get her."

"You saw who this person was?" Phillips asked.

"Yeah, mid-thirties, brown hair about six foot and a medium build. Drove a Ford town car with tinted windows," Finn answered.

"Would you recognize him again if you saw him?"

"Sure would. But what about Lexi? Where is she?" Finn questioned.

Sawyer couldn't answer. He sat completely immobilized and unable to function as his mind flicked through all the dreams he had for him and Lexi. It was as though his life flashed before his eyes. He pictured her walking towards him in her wedding dress with her father on her arm. Lexi with a swollen belly that carried their first child. Tears formed in his eyes and he knew they were falling from his face and there was not a damn thing he could do about it.

"Sawyer!" Finn bellowed. He was in front of him now and had grasped his shoulders. Sawyer didn't know how long he had been trying to get him out of his daze.

"Yeah…" he mumbled.

"Sawyer look at me!" Finn demanded, "Lexi needs you now. Not the man who loves her. She needs the Sheriff and the solider. You hear me?"

He was right and Sawyer knew he was, but he couldn't get his mouth to say the words. He thought back to their last conversation. She told him that she was in love with him and he had hesitated. Now, he felt his world shatter. He should have been honest with her. She should have told her that he loved her and wanted to spend the rest of his life with her. Suddenly the option was ripped out of his reach and he desperately wanted it back. He wanted her back and safe in his arms.

Phillips had stepped outside to make a couple of calls and Sawyer hoped he was calling in reinforcements from the FBI.

"I've spoken with Houston office and they're sending some men as soon as possible. In the meantime, we should retrace her steps and if someone can get me a map so I can take a look at what is around this place, that would help," Phillips directed.

Sawyer pushed down all the emotion and with an intense drive to find Lexi, he regained his composure. He picked up his phone and made contact with Parker. He didn't want to let the Scott's know what was happening because it would send them over the edge. Jack agreed and said that he didn't want to worry them if they could get Lexi back home where she belonged.

"Parker, Brant has Lexi and I need all deputies, but on shift and not at the McGuire Ranch right now," Sawyer barked into the phone.

"Yes, sir!" Parker responded.

"Did Lexi tell you much about Brant and his profile?" Phillips questioned.

"She told us some stuff about the trial and his crimes, but I don't recall a profile being thrown out there," Jack replied as he paced a hole in the floor in front of the couch.

"I've spent the last eighteen months learning everything I could about Brant. Like many serial killers, he has a routine and structure about how he kills and in what time frame. If Lexi told you about his crimes then you know that he holds his victims for approximately a week before he finally ends their torture," Phillips continued.

"So, we have a couple of days to find her?" Finn asked.

"If he sticks to his routine, yes. But he has gone off-script with Lexi. She's special to him for some reason. Probably because she challenged him and doesn't back down," Phillips added.

"In the meantime, he has her and is

doing God knows what..." Sawyer took a deep inhale to calm himself, "I can't think about that. We need her back now. How can we use the profile to narrow down a location where he could be holding his victims around Silverton?"

"I got a map here," Jack said, entering the house with a distraught Remi closely on his heels.

"She's gone?" Remi bellowed. His emotion was wild and manic. Sawyer knew how much his family cared for Lexi. She'd been the little girl that had visited on Sundays after church and the one they took turns pushing on the tire swing in their front yard.

Jack spread out the map on the long wooden dining table as every man surrounding it. Phillips took his time to examine the land around the town.

"Are there any old abandoned building or ranches around? Anything that would be isolated enough that someone wouldn't accidentally come upon it, but close enough to flee if needed?" Phillips asked.

"You're asking something there. We have a lot. Many of the ranches in Silverton and surrounding areas have suffered losses. There are hundreds or thousands of acres abandoned," Remi countered.

Parker and his other deputies arrived and quickly fell into the conversation.

"He would need somewhere he could confine people. Lock them in. Brant also liked a sterile environment to do his work. He was meticulous about cleanliness and ensuring that the only connection we had to his victims was his acknowledgement of the crimes," Phillips said, pacing back and forth with his hands on his hips. He'd taken off his blazer and had rolled up his white dress shirt.

"A barn would be too much open space. Especially if he wanted to keep her segregated. He hasn't had enough time to make any elaborate changes to the environment," Finn replied.

"We have noticed that he has made some mistakes since killing in Silverton," Sawyer mentioned.

This stopped Phillips in his tracks.

"What kind of mistakes?" he asked.

"We found DNA on one of the bodies that confirmed Brant as the killer. His letters have all been addressed to Lexi, whereas before he didn't address it to anyone. He simply took ownership of his "works"," Parker used his hands to provide air quotes to the word "works".

"From what I hear, we have a couple of options to begin searching," Remi commented, "if a barn is out of the picture, then we need to look at farms that had bunkers or places under the houses in case of tornados."

"No one would be able to hear her if she was deep underground like some of the old bunkers," Sawyer sighed.

"We have a make and model for the car Lexi was last seen in and a description of the fake Phillips. Sawyer, you should get your deputies tracking down all town cars in the area. Including rentals…If we can locate his accomplice then we might be able to break him," Finn said logically.

Sawyer turned to the ten deputies

all lined off in his living room. Some were dressed for duty and others had come in from their time off. He nodded to Parker and instructed them to follow Finn's direction. All members left to their tasks.

"I need him alive!" Sawyer yelled from his steps as he watched his employees fill into their different cars.

"Sawyer, do you have the key to the gun safes?" Remi asked, coming to stand next to him as he watched the cars fly down the road in a cloud of dust.

"Please tell me you didn't tell Aubrey," Sawyer asked.

"No, but she will eventually find out and then she's going to redden my hid. I filled in Jordan and she and Daisy are going to go stay with her and check in on the Scotts."

Sawyer didn't respond. Remi must have recognized the pain on his face because he clapped his brother's shoulders before turning to face him.

"We're going to get to her, Sawyer. You had my back when Aubrey was in trouble and we have yours now. I don't care whose ass I have to kick, we're bringing home our Lexi, okay?"

Our Lexi

She was a part of the family and a part of the ranch. Sawyer couldn't look at anything in the house or on the property that didn't remind him of her. She'd touched every aspect of his life and he had been blind. Nothing would be the same without her. Sawyer took one last glance at the tire swing that was held by the large oak tree his grandfather had planted. He could still see her smiling, innocent face as she threw her head back and laughed. Her long hair blew in the wind and the freckles prominent on her face from being in the sun.

He nodded and pulled the gun safe keys from his pocket. He waved it in front of his brother.

"Let's go get our girl," Sawyer announced before walking into the house with Remi and making his way downstairs to the gun safe.

He'd get her back by any means necessary.

Chapter 22

LEXI / SAWYER

Lexi was roughly jolted out of her sleep by the sound of the metal door slamming shut. She quickly went on alert and pushed herself up against the wall. Standing before her was the man she had believed to be Agent Phillips. He'd disposed of the fancy suit and was wearing simple jeans and shirt. He glared at her from his post in the doorway.

"What do you want?" Lexi snapped.

Lexi saw his jaw grind in anger. He wasn't used to people talking to him disrespectfully. Well, screw it. If she was going to kick the bucket, she was going out her own way. Her sadness and grief had quickly morphed into anger. The man slammed a metal tray on the desk.

"So starvation is Brant's limit?" she scoffed.

"Eat," the man grunted before he turned and slammed the door behind him.

Lexi was starving, but she wouldn't put it past Brant to poison the food. She needed to get out of the shackles that were binding her to the room. If she could get free, perhaps she could catch one of them by surprise when they came back for the tray.

Lexi eyed the tray to see what had been included and whether anything to help with her goal. There was a plastic mug which held what looked to be water, a plastic plate with a knife and fork. Also plastic, but Lexi though that she could get it to a point. If she could perhaps it would inflict some harm.

Butter.

There was butter. She quickly opened the small package and spread the butter across her wrist. The grease coated her skin and despite the bleeding and wounds, she kept trying to get her wrist free. She exhausted herself in her attempts to free her hand with butter. All she succeeded in doing was greasing her arm.

Lexi knew that her thumb was the issue. She could easily fit her slim fingers through the shackle if her thumb bone wasn't as prominent. She slid down against the wall, frustrated and angry. She knew she would have to take drastic measures to get herself out of the situation she was in. But she also knew that she wouldn't leave Carly.

Carly.

Lexi hadn't heard her scream for a while now and she was concerned that Brant had ended her torture. She couldn't think about it or she would lose all will to get out of this hell. She needed to get out. Lexi eyed the desk and noticed that it hadn't been bolted down. She needed out of the shackles. She was at Brant and his accomplice's mercy as long as she was confined.

Lexi closed her eyes and sighed. A sob formed in her throat and she choked it back. She knew she needed out of the chains and the only way to do that was to break a bone or two in her hand. She took a deep calming breath. She ripped a part of her shirt and rolled it as a gag for her mouth. She wouldn't be able to hold back a scream from the pain. She hoped the fabric would help muffle the cry she knew would escape her body.

She shuffled over to the metal desk and as quietly as possible moved it closer so that she could get a better handle on it. The desk was heavy and she was sure that Brant selected heavy furniture in hopes that she wouldn't be able to lift it. Using the one-gallon bucket designated as her toilet, she flipped the desk on its side slowly and using the bucket perched it in between the desk and the floor, so it was holding the desk and she could kick the bucket out and have the slam down on her hand.

She placed her hand under the opening and hoped that with enough momentum to break the bone in one drop. Lexi put the cloth in her mouth and prepared her foot for the kick. She said a silent prayer and thought about Sawyer. She needed to get out there for him. If nothing else, she couldn't let him find her the way the other victims had been found.

Lexi closed her eyes and took a deep breath before kicking the bucket. Pain radiated through her arm and she bit into the cloth as tears flew from her eyes. She looked down at her hand and saw the bone protruding at an odd angle. With some additional pain to get her hand out of the shackle, Lexi grimaced but pushed through until she got her hand free.

She spat out the cloth and wrapped up her hand the best she could. She knew she'd need to put everything back where it was for when the lunch lady came back. Lexi took the metal tray and sat next to the chains on the wall with her injuries hand hidden. She'd use the tray to hit him over the head when he came to collect.

She needed to fight for her life. She needed to get out and get help for Carly.

The lock on the outside of the door clicked and Lexi moved into position and thanked her father and brother for their tips on fighting. Lexi knew her legs were the strongest part of her body now since her left hand was damaged.

Psychopath number two moved toward her and bent in front of her to collect the tray. Once he was closed enough she did exactly what her father taught her. She went for the family jewels. Striking out with her right hand she punched those suckers with all her strength. He groaned before he fell to the floor. Lexi rose and made a run for the door, but he grabbed her ankle and yanked. She fell to the floor but kicked out with her legs and managed to get a solid hit to his face. She heard a crunch and he released his grip on her leg. She flew to her feet and scrambled out the door, closing it shut behind her.

Now, where the fuck was she?

The fluorescent lighting was harsh and caused her to squint as she got her bearings. She took a chance and went left in hopes of getting out of whatever cell or bunker she was held captive in. Running as fast and as quietly as possible, she worked her way around the halls until she found another door. Behind the door was a ladder that led to an opening hatch in the roof. Using one hand she climbed the ladder until she got to the top and turned the wheel to unlock the opening. She heard the click and struggled to push the latch open. She heard footsteps approaching as she climbed out of the hole. She must have tripped a silent alarm when she opened the latch.

Getting to her feet, she found herself in an open field. She didn't recognize the area. She took a breath and hoped that the cover of darkness would help her if Brant ran after her. And she was sure he would. She fled as fast as she could to the tree line. The glanced over her shoulder to see Brant lifting the latch.

"LEXI!" he bellowed. She kept running and refused to look back again as she heard his footsteps behind her.

She needed to getaway.

SAWYER

Night had fallen and the knot in Sawyer's gut was wound uptight. They were doing everything that they could to locate Lexi and bring her home. He sat in the living room as Phillips talked with his superiors, Remi and Finn checked and re-checked the weapons they had. Finn had been a sniper when he was in the Rangers and could shoot from at least five hundred yards. He would keep a level head in a crisis and that's what he needed covering his back.

The rear door slapped open and in walked t Aubrey with his two sisters in tow. Aubrey immediately moved towards Sawyer and wrapped her arms around his neck.

"I'm so sorry Sawyer," she sobbed into his neck.

Sawyer wrapped his arms around his sister in law and rubbed her back. His heart broke into a million pieces. Aubrey was a strong woman and she knew how to hold her own, but she felt things deeply. Sawyer eyed his brother from over her shoulder and glanced at him for assistance with his wife.

Remi gentle pulled Aubrey from Sawyer and sat on the love seat with her in his arms as he comforted her.

"We're going to find her, firecracker," Remi said holding her face in his hand gently. Aubrey let out an unladylike sniff before she hugged her husband and placed a kiss on his lips.

"I love you, but if you don't come back to me I'll resurrect you just to kill you myself, got it?" Aubrey said firmly jabbing her little finger into his chest. Remi just grabbed her hand and kissed her fingers.

"There is nothing in this world that could keep me from you. But Lex is family and this is what we do to protect the ones we love," he assured her and she nodded before giving him another passionate kiss and rising.

She pressed a kiss to his cheek and whispered, "I need you to come back too. I wouldn't be able to cope if we lost the three of you." Tears welled in her eyes as she moved to kiss Finn before heading out the door.

Daisy stood firm while Jordan kissed her family and headed out after Aubrey.

"I'm coming with you," she announced.

"No fucking way!" the three of them bellowed in unison.

She rolled her eyes but shot them a glare that said there was going to fight. And that she would do whatever the hell she wanted, so it was best to just give in.

"I'm going. It's not up for discussion. So you can either have a come to Jesus moment about my involvement and accept it, or someone handcuffs me and locks me in a room," she offered.

"Phillips, you got a spare set of cuffs?" Remi questioned. Within minutes Remi had them in hand and was making his way to Daisy.

"Do you think I've never gotten myself out of handcuffs before?" She challenged with a smirk.

Finn shook his head and made a sour face, "Jesus Daisy, no one needs to know about your fucked up fetish shit."

Sawyer sighed as he pulled his sister into a hug, "Dais, I know you want to help and I get it. But my head is barely functioning now at the thought of what Lexi is going through. I can't have you taking up space there too. I need to know you're safe, Daisy Duke."

Daisy glanced away from him and he knew he'd pulled on her strings. She melted into his hug and sighed.

"Okay..." she hesitated, "go bring our girl home, Sawyer." With that, she kissed and hugged them and told them she loved them before returning to Remi's home by the lake.

"So, that's settled..." Phillips said, "let's go over the plan and teams. We have a lot of ground to cover and not a lot of time."

Everyone gathered around the map and it was agreed that Sawyer and Finn would team up given their training and Remi would go with Phillips and Jack.

Finn got his sniper rifle and a handgun, which he slipped into his shoulder holster. Sawyer did the same and he had to repeatedly rub his chest due to the void his heartfelt.

They started with the old Johnson farm. The family owned a cattle farm years ago, but when the elders passed away the children had no interest in the place or the life. The land sat unoccupied for years. They parked on the side of the road and made their way to the main structure.

"I think Billy Johnson said that his parents had a nuclear bunker in the basement from the 60s," Finn said as they walked the surrounding structure. They pushed the back along either side of the door before Finn reached over and opened the door. Sawyer moved in flanked by Finn. Finn headed to the hayloft and Sawyer cleared the main area of the barn.

"Clear," he shouted.

Sawyer's phone chimed in his pocket. They had exchanged numbers to check in when they cleared a location.

Parker: A resident ID'd the car heading north   on Route 86 this afternoon.

Phillips: We're on the other end and just cleared the Thompson location. Moving to the empty glass factory now.

Sawyer: We're closer. We have the Saunders farm that way and will clear the location.

There were hundreds of thousands of acres in the area and he knew they wouldn't get to search every spot. He felt hopeless and desperate. Finn and Sawyer made their way to the Saunder's farm just off of Route 86. They ran a small milk operation and had a barn and a warehouse for storage. They spent several months a year with their grandchildren up north and their residence would be vacated until they returned.

They entered the house and a tingle coursed through his body and the hair on his arm stood at attention. The Saunders had been gone for a month, but someone continued to get their newspaper. The two-storey farmhouse was cleared and Finn joined Sawyer in the kitchen to make an entrance to the basement.

The light was on which immediately piqued Sawyer's interest as they descended the stairs. Sawyer noted that it looked as though someone was doing laundry.

"Sawyer," Finn said looking at a small desk in the corner.

He moved to see what had caught his brother's interest. The stationary on the desk was the same as the one that was left with each of Brant's victims since he was in Silverton.

"He was here," Sawyer acknow-ledged.

"According to Phillips, he took tro-phies and kept them with him," Finn said.

Sawyer nodded and they started to tear the place apart. Underneath the stairs was a small backpack that had been stuffed out of sight. Sawyer opened the bag and pulled out a medium size box. His stomach sank as he thought about what kind of tro-phies Brant would have. He inhaled a deep breath before he flipped open the box. In-side he found polaroids of his victims. Ter-ror was etched across their faces. They were all chained or shackled. Sawyer felt his stomach urge as he flicked through the pic-tures. Then his eyes landed on one of Lexi. She appeared to be unconscious and laying on a dirty mattress with a chain around her left wrist.

"Shit," Finn muttered from over his shoulder.

Sawyer tried not to think the worse. If she wasn't with them anymore he was convinced that he would feel the loss in his soul. But he held on hope that his smart mouth woman would be able to hold on until he found her.

Sawyer put everything back the way he found it, "We need everything in place in case he returns. If he does I want to follow him to wherever he is holding Lexi and Carly."

"We should search the perimeter. I haven't seen the bunker that was alleged to have been here, so maybe it's in another part of the farm," Finn agreed.

They both stepped out of the house. The calm of the night was juxtaposed with the raging storm in his heart. The stars hung high in the clear sky and it was quiet and peaceful. Sawyer turned his face to the stars.

"Old man, if you're listening. I need your help here. I need to find her. Help me find her," he begged.

"Sawyer!" Finn yelled and his scream had him running towards him at the rear of the house.

There he found a latch that had been covered up with years of ground. They quickly turned the lever and after some tugging, they were able to get the latch open. They lowered themselves into the tunnel below. The darkness encompassed them and they waited for their sight to adjust. Sawyer grabbed his brother's wrist possessively.

"We don't split," he ordered. Finn nodded his agreement and gave the hand signal to move forward.

They spotted light at the far end of the tunnel. As they came closer to the light, they heard whimpers from a woman. Sawyer turned towards a door that had a brief window in it and gazed inside. There he saw a woman in only her underwear, curled in the fetal position with her back away from him. He couldn't tell if it was Lexi, but regardless, she needed to get out of there. Sawyer went to open the door only to find it locked.

"Fuck," he cursed.

"Move aside," Finn demanded as he cranked a flashlight and pulled a small lock picking kit from his   pocket. In seconds, Finn had the lock snapped open.

"Where did you learn that?" Sawyer

questioned before Finn pushed open the door.

"Like our sister, I've also found myself in handcuffs," he confirmed.

They made entry to the room with weapons raised. Once the place was cleared, Sawyer moved to the injured woman who laid whimpering on the floor. He approached cautiously as he could see a variety of cuts, bruises and burns all over her body. As he got closer he realized the woman wasn't Lexi.

"Carly," he said gently. Her eyes opened as far as they could, "Let's get you out of here okay? You're safe with us okay?"

"Chains," was all she was able to mutter.

"Finn, pick this lock," he commanded and he wasted no time getting the bonds off the woman's wrist. Once the locks were off, Finn bent and pulled Carly into his chest and Sawyer moved forward to cover. Sawyer tried hard to look around the space, but he failed. The woman had been chained and hanging around here was a variety of torture instruments. They needed to get her out of the hell and get her medical attention.

"Get her to the surface," he ordered.

"We said we wouldn't split, Sawyer," Finn barked.

"She needs help, Finn. Go! I'll be fine!" He said while moving down the hall. He heard his brother grunt his annoyance before he moved towards the exit they had just entered. Sawyer moved slitty through the long narrow corridors. He came to another door and peeked inside through the small window in the door.

The room was dark and he strained to see if there was anything in the room. Then out of nowhere, a man popped up banging on the door. His nose was bleeding and his eyes were lit with fire. Sawyer recognized him as the fake Agent Phillips and glared at the man.

"Where is she, you piece of shit?" he screamed.

"How the fuck would I know? That bitch attacked me and locked me in here," he gritted.

Inside Sawyer was proud that his

woman hadn't given up hope and had fought her way out. Lexi wasn't the type to sit around and wait for someone to come to find her. She created her own way. Sawyer smirked and made his way down the hall. He ignored the profanities yelled at him from the sick fuck in the locked room. He'd be secure in there for now and he needed to get to Lexi. He'd been in the whole bunker and hadn't found Brant, so he believed that when Lexi was able to flee that Brant followed her.

He climbed up the ladder on the other side of the door and made his exit. He saw an ambulance and police in the distance. He yelled out and Finn ran toward him. Lexi had to have left through that exit. He stood above the ground and looked around the space in a circle. What would she do?

The trees... She'd seek cover from trees. She'd have a better chance of survival with the coverage and hiding places of the green evergreens.

"She wasn't there and neither was Brant. I think she made for the tree line," Sawyer said to his brother. That's when he heard it.

"Lexi! I'm going to find you!" a voice from the trees.

"Jesus Christ," Sawyer took off running in the direction of the sounds. Before he made it to the first-ever green the sounds of a gunshot boomed through the calm night sky. His blood ran cold and he picked up the pace in hopes of finding Lexi or Brant. Once he got his hands on that psycho, he would kill him.

Chapter 23

LEXI

Lexi ran through the darkness and prayed that Brant had a poor sense of direction. She'd always loved the solitude of the woods in Silverton, but tonight it was working against her. Her breath rushed out of her body as she sped through the trees. Her hand throbbed and her legs were starting to tire.

She hid behind a tall oak to catch her breath and figure out where she was. She listened for any sudden movements in the distance that would tell her if Brant was close. A branch snapped in the distance and Lexi covered her mouth to muffle the sound of her ragged breathing.

"Lexi, come on. You know I'll find you where ever you are," Brant sang through the trees. He was close and she needed to put a larger distance between them. Lexi took in a large gulp of air before pushing off the tree and sprinting. She ran in between trees in hopes to prevent Brant from spotting her.

Her heart pounded in her chest and sweat dripped down her forehead and neck. She hated the idea of running from any problem, but in her current condition, she wouldn't be able to fight off Brant. Fleeing was the only option and Carly was counting on her to get help. If she was even still alive. She glanced behind her to see if she could spot Brant gaining on her, but she stumbled and fell to the ground. Dirt crumbled into her face and she felt the warm trickle of blood down her knee. She scrambled to her feet and started running but a gunshot boomed through the woods and hit a tree not far from her head. She let out a yelp but kept running, zig-zagging around the ever-greens.

"Lexi!" a familiar voice screamed into the darkness.

Sawyer.

Shit! He needed to keep quiet or

Brant wouldn't hesitate to take him out. Lexi couldn't live with the thought of him hurt because of her. He'd been hurting for ten years because of her accident and the guilt had tarnished a piece of his soul. She wouldn't let him carry the burden of her life.

She heard movement around her but couldn't be sure if it was Brant or Sawyer. One determined to take her life and one was her life. She saw a clearing up ahead and took the chance. She ran towards the grassy field in hopes of finding Sawyer and others to help. Once she made it to the clearing she turned around only to find that she was still surrounded by trees and to one side was a small rock wall.

"Sawyer!" she screamed taking the chance that he would be able to get to her before Brant.

Frantically she searched the trees hoping that she would be able to lure one of the men to where she was standing. If Brant found her, she would try and delay the inevitable. Her blood trumped through her veins and her chest rose and fell at a rapid speed. Her hair stuck to her face as she moved her head quickly trying to see into the trees.

BANG!

BANG!

Gunshots.

There was a rustling in the far corner of the trees and Lexi stood still in the middle of the clearing. Her eyes landed on Sawyer who was walking slowly out of the tree line. Her heart raced and a smile broke across her face as she made to run towards him he called out.

"No Lexi! Stay there!"

It was then she noticed a wet spot on his arm and he winced as something from behind pushed him forward. Sawyer fell to his knees and behind him came Brant. From the depths of the darkness, he rose with a gun in his hand and pointed at Sawyer.

"NO!" Lexi screamed.

"Lexi, stay back!" Sawyer growled.

Brant eyed them both before he concluded that they knew each other. His grin widened when he saw the pain in her eyes.

"Well, isn't this lovely!" he chirped

as he walked to the side of Sawyer adjusting the position of the gun to push against his temple.

"You two know each other pretty well I take it?" he sneered.

Lexi's stomach dropped and the overwhelming feeling of grief stole her breath.

"Let him go Brant!" she hissed. "He means nothing to you. It's me you want!"

"Lexi!" Sawyer bellowed.

"Oh my, what a wonderful treat! You love him?" Brant questioned with a quizzical expression.

Lexi didn't answer and Brant grinned before he pushed in on Sawyer's wounded arm. He cried out in pain and Lexi's heart broke.

"Stop it! Let him go!" Lexi screamed and advanced closer.

"Answer me, Lexi! Is this the man you love?" Brant hissed.

Their eyes met across the grassy field and tears escaped down her cheeks. Everything she wanted for her life flashed before her. Her wedding day, her first child, her first niece or nephew all came to the forefront. And all of those memories she stood next to the man she loved. Sawyer. Her life was nothing without him. She couldn't live or see a future without him in it.

"Y-Yes…" she whispered.

Brant clapped his hands together in glee, "Oh my! And you, do you love her?" He pointed the gun to Sawyer's head and pressed it to his temple causing Sawyer to flinch.

"Take me!" Lexi cried. "Take me, please!"

Brant's head quickly swivelled in her direction and Sawyer dropped his head and closed his eyes. She wouldn't see him hurt because of her anymore. If she had to offer up her life for his, there was no question about what she would do. Brant's smile widened and he chuckled like an evil villain in a superhero movie.

"Come to me, my pet and I'll let your lover live."

Lexi wept but refused to back down. She would do whatever she needed to keep him safe. He deserved a happy life and a future. Lexi had already beaten death once and she knew a second time wasn't likely.

Lexi lifted her chin high and slowly stepped towards the love of her life and the end of her life. Every step caused her heart to ache, but she knew she was doing the right thing. Sawyer wouldn't be in this situation if it wasn't for her. As she approached, Brant reached for her. She couldn't move her gaze from Sawyer as she reached out and grabbed his hand. Once in his grasp, Brant pulled her in front of him and placed the gun to her head.

"You won't get far, Brant," Sawyer threatened and Lexi saw the pure animalistic rage on his face.

"Oh, I wasn't planning to get very far," he cooed before he raised the gun in Sawyer's direction and aimed.

"No!" Lexi yelled as she reached across and knocked the gun from his hand. Brant grabbed her by the hair and yanked her back against him. The gun fell into the grass but Brant came prepared and whipped out a switchblade.

"Bitch!" he screamed before he

plunged the knife into Lexi's thigh. She crumpled to the ground as the blood oozed from her wound. The last thing she saw before darkness swept into her vision was Brant standing over her with the knife raised.

SAWYER

Sawyer's heart stopped the minute Lexi offered herself up to the psychopath with the gun. He'd been focused on getting to Lexi that he let his guard down and Brant was able to graze his arm with a bullet.

Sawyer jumped into action when Lexi knocked the gun from Brant, but he wasn't quick enough to get to them before he stabbed her. Sawyer watched the colour drain from her face as she crumpled to the ground. Brant stood over her with the knife raised ready to end her life, but Sawyer was quicker. He sped at the man and plunged into him taking him to the ground. Brant was surprisingly strong and was an equal match for Sawyer. They rolled around the grassy field as both struggled to get the upper hand. Sawyer swung a right hook into his jaw and watched his head bob back. He kept pounding his fist into Brant's face until his eyes rolled and his head bounced around. Once Sawyer was satisfied that he was unconscious, he moved to Lexi.

Her skin had turned a sickly colour grey and her beautiful hazel eyes were closed. He noticed the cloth around her left hand and the blood from the chains on her wrist. The stab wound was bleeding heavily and Sawyer feared that Brant had struck the main vein and that she could bleed out. Sawyer yanked off his belt and wrapped it around her upper thigh tightly.

"Lexi," he cried once the belt was in place, "open those beautiful eyes for me, sweetheart."

He checked her over for any other wounds and checked for a pulse. It was weak but it was there. She needed medical attention immediately and there wasn't a minute to spare. Every second they were away from help was a second that she drifted farther into unconsciousness. Sawyer bent to pulled Lexi into his arms, but the sound of a gunshot floated through the air.

Sawyer turned in time to see Brant's eyes fall to his chest where a bullet had penetrated. His hand was raised with a knife and he was walking towards them. He dropped to his knees as the blood-soaked his shirt. Another shot rang out and this time it landed right between his eyes and jolted his body back to the floor of the field. Sawyer looked up and around and caught the glimmer of a scope from the top of the rock wall.

Finn.

God, he was proud to have siblings who he could count on to have his back. Sawyer gently tugged Lexi into his arms and rushed out of the field. She fell limp in his arms and his heart clenched.

"I can't lose you, baby" he whispered.

Finn greeted him at the base of the cliff and was carrying his sniper rifle. He'd always known that his brother was a damn good Ranger and sniper, but to see it first-hand made him beyond proud of his baby brother. Finn flanked him as they ran towards the farmhouse.

"You're bleeding," Finn huffed.

"I know," Sawyer gritted.

"Let me take her, Sawyer" Finn demanded.

"Not gonna happen, brother" Sawyer growled. He understood why his brother would want that. Sawyer was injured and Finn wasn't. It made sense, but it would be a cold day in hell before he would part from Lexi.

When the flashing lights of the ambulance and patrol cars came into view, Sawyer breathed a sigh of relief. Jack ran to greet them concern etched across his face as he saw his sister lying lifeless in Sawyer's arms.

"God no," he huffed and fell to his knees. Finn grabbed him and carried him towards the ambulance.

"She's still with us, Jack," Finn assured him.

Sawyer ran straight for the ambulance and laid her on a gurney. The paramedics worked around him setting her up with monitors and IVs. He glanced at the door to see his brothers and Jack watching and feeling helpless.

"Jack, I'm going with her. Meet me at the hospital," he ordered and all three men nodded.

"Her pulse is weak. She's lost a lot of blood," the paramedic said before she hit the roof and the ambulance took off towards the hospital. Sawyer held her hand the whole way and waited for some sign of life. Her breath was ragged and her colour hadn't changed from the sickly grey she had in the field.

He caressed her cheek hoping for any movement from her. If nothing else he just needed to touch her to know that she was still here. He gently moved in and placed a kiss to her forehead, lingering to memorize the feel of her and the smell of her. He rested his head by her ear and took a deep breath. He was numb. He couldn't feel the bullet wound, but the ache in his heart was torture.

"I love you, Lexi. I love you so much. You can't leave me. I need you. You hear me, Lexi. I can't live without you so I need you to pull through okay?" he pleads as he pulled back.

"We're here, Sheriff" the paramedic prompted just before the door flung open and they were hustled inside.

Sawyer gripped her hand until he couldn't anymore and the staff had to pry him away from her. The nurses had finally set him up on a bed where they treated his bullet wound. He already knew it was a graze, but they weren't letting him leave without seeing it treated. Once he was cleared he moved to the waiting area outside the OR.

He exited the door and was struck with a force of nature. His sisters had bombarded him with love and affection as they cried.

"I'm okay," he whispered as he wrapped his arms around all three of them. Remi managed to pull his wife off of him and held her in his arms. "Jo-Jo?" Sawyer whispered to his eldest sister. She was always a pillar of strength so seeing her cry was a sure sign that they were beyond worried.

"Y-Yeah?" she said as she lifted her face from his chest and stared at him with her bloodshot eyes.

"Can you do something for me?" he ran his thumb under her cheek to wipe away her tears.

"Anything," she answered without hesitation.

He kissed her forehead, "Can you find out anything about Lex? You got some pull here right?" She nodded her head and pulled away. She turned to walk down the hall and came face to face with Chase. He looked frazzled and unkempt, a crease formed in his usually soft face. They stood still staring at each other for a brief moment. Neither certain how to move forward.

"Jordan," Chase muttered as he reached for her. Tears flew down her face and everyone stood silent waiting for her response. She was in a fragile state and Chase had always been a sour topic for her. Despite their broken hearts, both of them still cared for each other. Jordan met his gaze and he moved to wrap his arms around her.

Behind them, a frantic Mr and Mrs Scott stormed through the hospital doors. Jack greeted them before they could freak out.

"Where is she? Is she okay?" Jessica cried in her son's arms. Baxter quickly moved towards Sawyer and clasped his shoulder. He looked as though he'd aged twenty years in twenty-four hours.

"Son, tell me what's happening with my baby," he begged.

Sawyer settled in and went through the entire story with his family and Lexi's family. Once he had thoroughly explained the situation to all of them, he turned to Baxter and Jessica.

"I couldn't keep her safe. I'm sorry," he confessed.

With that, Jessica rose from her seat and fell to her knees in front of him. She grabbed his hands firmly but in a motherly way that Sawyer had almost forgotten. It'd been so long since his mother had been around and Jessica reminded him of everything that was great about mothers.

"Sawyer, look at me," she demanded and he followed her order. Like her daughter, Sawyer had a hard time denying the woman anything.

"This is not your fault. Lexi is strong and she will come through this and we will be there for her every step of the way. Just like last time."

A silent tear slowly trickled down his cheek and she reached up to brush it away and held his jaw in her small delicate hand.

"You love her," she announced.

"More than life itself," he admitted. He cautiously met her gaze and saw the tears in her eyes and the smile that danced along her face. "And with your permission, I'd like to marry her if she'll have me."

Chapter 24

LEXI

Lexi's eyes were crusted shut and her ability to move was limited. There was a recurring beeping in the darkness and each breath scratched against her throat roughly. She was groggy and everything in sight was blurred. She heard the movement of someone else in the room and she tried to see who it was. But her eyes shut close.

"P-P- Pain..." she managed to huff through the pain. Her throat was on fire and her voice sounded like she'd been smoking for a hundred years. A nurse gently touched her shoulder to provide some comfort.

"I'll get you something for pain, Ms Scott," the nurse said before she scurried off. Lexi didn't know if she returned or not because she was swept back into unconsciousness. She woke again on her own and her head didn't feel as dizzy but she desperately needed to get her hands on some water. She licked her lips to ease her dry chapped lips.

She took note of her body and her surroundings. Her left hand was in a cast, which she expected considering the injury she had inflicted. She was in a scratchy hospital gown and fortunately was still wearing underwear. Using her right hand she pushed off the blanket to look at her leg. It was bandaged but she was able to move her toes.

Movement in the dark corner caught her attention. Slung over a hospital chair with his head rested against the wall was Sawyer. He slept with his arms crossed and his body stiff. Passed out on the floor beside him was her brother. He looked like shit. His hair was completely mussed and there was an unknown stain on his shirt and he wasn't wearing pants.

She chuckled briefly before a pair of green eyes captured her attention. Finn. He stood in the doorway of the dark room.

His beautiful green eyes darkened by circles and lines which screamed that he wasn't sleeping. He stepped forward and pressed a loving kiss to her forehead. He then moved over to where his brother was sleeping and grasped his shoulder. Sawyer stumbled awake and looked up his brother.

"She's awake," he said softly.

Sawyer was out of his seat and at her side before she could blink. He sat on the side of the bed and wrapped his arms around her. Tears engulfed her eyes and she didn't fight them off. She needed to be in his arms and she needed his strength. He nuzzled into her neck and Lexi felt the beat of his heart in his chest against hers.

"I love you, Lexi. I love you so God damn much and I don't want to live another day without you knowing it," he said into her neck. He pulled back briefly and their foreheads met as Lexi closed her eyes.

"Sawyer, you don't have to say it just because I did..." she managed. He got to his feet quickly and paced the room as Jack and Finn stood to the side and watched in amusement.

"Jesus Lexi," he cursed while running a hand through his messy hair, "I love you and not because of what happened. I should have told you that I loved you when you said it that morning, but I was scared."

"Scared of what?" she demanded.

"That I wouldn't be enough. That one day you'd wake up and fly back to New York and I'd be left in a pile of cow shit crying," he yelled.

"Sweet Jesus..." Finn said from the corner, his hand raised to muffle his laughter.

"Don't you have somewhere else to be right now?" Sawyer barked at his brother.

"Nope..." he replied with a full-on smile on his face.

"Son of a ..." he muttered.

"Sawyer," Lexi sighed, "I would never do that to you. We've spent ten years pushing each other away. There is nothing back in New York that would ever be more important than a life with you."

Sawyer pushed a chair up to her hospital bed and gently took her right hand, careful not to touch the IV. "I almost lost you," he whispered before kissing her hand. Lexi pushed forward and captured his lips in a sweet and longing kiss.

"And that's our cue to leave," Finn and Jack groaned.

Just after they left, there was a knock on the door and a young woman appeared in her long white coat. She was about Lexi's age and had long blond hair and beautiful eyes. The couple broke apart but Sawyer remained by her side.

"Nice to see you're up, Ms Scott. I'm Doctor James and I've been taking care of you," she acknowledged with a smile. "I want to go over what happened medically and your recuperation process," she continued.

"Okay..." Lexi agreed. Dr James eyed Sawyer speculatively, "It's okay Doctor James. Whatever I need to know Sawyer can hear."

She nodded before she went through the surgery on her leg and the break of her hand. Lexi had lost a lot of blood and fortunately, they received a huge influx of people from the community who wanted to donate blood.

"You're a strong woman, Lexi. Especially a woman in your condition, I was expecting much worse," she said.

Lexi went through her brain as to what she could mean by her "condition". Lexi had been perfectly healthy before the incident unless she was talking about her previous injury.

"Oh, my previous injury from the car accident doesn't have any physical impacts now. I wouldn't say it's a condition," Lexi countered.

Doctor James glanced up from her clipboard, "Lexi, that's not the condition I was speaking about."

Lexi's mind went into overdrive. Could it be that they discovered some condition or disease when she was in the OR or during this hospital stay?

"What do you mean? Is there something wrong with me beside the leg and hand?" Lexi questioned, anxiety prickled at the back of her neck, but Sawyer moved closer and wrapped his hand around the base of her neck. Massaging the muscles in light gentle strokes.

Doctor James put her chart on the end of her bed and a smile crossed her face, "No Lexi, nothing like that. But we did find out during blood work that you're about five to six weeks pregnant."

Sawyer's touch ceased and Lexi's heart jerked causing the heart monitors to beep rapidly. Lexi's hand went to her stomach and a different type of fear took hold.

"Oh God, is the baby okay?" she gasped.

"He or she is fine. We completed an ultrasound while you were in recovery and the baby, much like its mama is strong," she smiled and picked up her chart before turning to the door. "You'll be discharged in the morning and congratulations."

Lexi couldn't hold back the tears as she rubbed her belly. There was another human being in there. She was going to be someone's mother. And Sawyer would be...

"Sawyer," she said gently as she wasn't sure what kind of reaction to suspect from him. Sawyer was great with children, but they hadn't even talked about the future and now there was a baby.

"Are you okay?" she asked reluctantly as Sawyer stared out into the distance without blinking. He was in shock. Definitely in shock. There was no way he could stay silent that long.

"A baby…" he whispered, "we're having a baby." Then he unleashed a smile that brightened the room. A megawatt smile that Lexi had never seen him share before and her heart bloomed with hope. He grabbed her face and kissed her passionately. "I love you, Lex," he whispered against her lips.

Then he gradually moved his face down to her belly and placed a kiss above her belly button. "And I love you peanut. We're so excited to meet you little one," he said quietly.

Lexi had never been so happy. Brant was dead. Sawyer was in her arms and she was about to be a mother. Her life had taken such a turn for the better and she wondered whether her Nana knew it all along. Maybe she forced her to return to heal her broken heart, or maybe she knew that everything she needed to complete her heart was in Silverton. Her parents. Her brother. The ranch. And the cowboy who broke her heart and was the only one who could complete it.

Épilogue

2 YEARS LATER...

"You ready for this, Sawyer?" Remi asked over the top of his beer as they sat on the front porch of their family home.

"There's no going back once the ring is on your finger," Finn continued from his other side.

Sawyer smiled, "Y'all trying to talk me out of it?"

"Hell no! She's the best woman you've ever had. But if you're not going to follow through, I might give it a go," Finn jabbed.

"That's it," Sawyer said as he stood and grabbed the scruff of his brother's neck, pulling him into a headlock. Before he knew it, they were on the grass rolling around.

"Take it back!" Sawyer yelled from on top of Finn's back and twisting his arm until he tapped out. Both laughed in between stunts, but Sawyer wasn't letting him get away with that dig.

"HEY!" a strong feminine voice bellowed from the steps.

"Uh oh," they muttered together. Sawyer released his brother and they both stood. Miss Martha wasted no time stalking to them and grabbing them both by the ear.

"Ow, shit," Finn cussed.

"What have I told you two about roughhousing?" she drawled.

"That we're bad examples," Sawyer muttered.

"Exactly, but you're also going to get your clothes covered in grass stains," she muttered before sauntering into the house. Sawyer strolled back to his seat where Remi held out his beer.

"Babe!" Aubrey called from inside the house before sticking her head out the screen door.

"Yes firecracker," Remi answered.

"Do you think you could help me?"

she cooed.

"With what?" he asked.

A blush ran up Aubrey's cheeks as she hesitated to answer, "My dress, Remington."

"Gotta go, boys," Remi smiled as he sprinted to the door and a feminine yelp was heard as Sawyer suspected Remi had tossed his wife over his shoulder.

Emma and Leo appeared from around the corner of the house with Jordan. All were dressed in their fancy Sunday clothes. Jordan had on her bridesmaid dress and Emma her flower girl get up. Leo was going to be one of Sawyer's groomsmen and looked dapper in his suit. Jordan was carrying a squirming little boy who was eager to get down.

"Hunter, you aren't getting down on the grass. You'll ruin your little suit," Jordan said firmly.

"Nooooo! Hate suit!" he grumbled and pushed out his little bottom lip in a pout.

Jordan rolled her eyes before she got to the step and put Hunter down. He ran over to Sawyer and hopped into his arms. He was fourteen months old and still learning to run, but his walking had improved. Hunter turned in Sawyer's arms and pointed out towards the farmland.

"Grass!" he declared.

"You heard Jo Jo, Hunter. Your mother will kill me if you get dirty," Sawyer sighed as the baby pout worked him over.

"WE'RE READY!" Daisy bellowed from inside the house and they all made their way to the rear of the house where guests were already sat and the priest was already standing at the makeshift altar

Sawyer carried Hunter with him as he moved to take his place at the end of the altar. Daisy had done an amazing job getting things together.

Fifty white garden chairs were placed on either side of a long white runner of satin. Mini lights had been strung from the tears and flowers decorated the aisle and altar.

"Grandma!" Hunter cried from his side as he spotted Jessica coming towards them. She smiled and blew them a kiss before taking her seat in the front row. She looked amazing in a dusty rose dress.

Once everyone had taken their seats, the groomsmen came to join Sawyer's side. All dressed in light blue Levi's, white button-downs and a vest, they all looked like sensible men. Brett clapped him on the shoulder before swinging in to ruffle Hunter's light brown hair.

Sawyer turned to the little menace in his arms, "Now, you remember what Daddy said about staying by him when mommy walks towards us, right?"

He exaggerated his nod and put a huge grin on his face.

"So if I let you down, you're going to hold my hand and stay by me, right?" Sawyer reminded.

"Yep!" Hunter affirmed. Sawyer didn't believe it. The child had been pushing the limits since he was born.

The music started and Sawyer put him down and wrapped his little hand into his. He watched as his sisters walked down the aisle with bright smiles on their faces.

Then everyone stood and time stood still as Lexi and Baxter came to a stand at the end of the aisle.

"Mommy!" Hunter called.

"Mommy is coming to us remember?" Sawyer directed adjusting his hold on the little mini troublemaker.

Lexi smiled brightly up the aisle and kissed her father before joining his and their son at the altar. Baxter shook his hand and joined his wife in the front row.

"I love you," Sawyer said.

"I love you," she replied.

"Love me!" Hunter cried from his side causing laughter to erupt in the audience.

"Come here trouble," Sawyer said lifting him into his arms. Lexi placed a kiss to his head before they turned to face the priest.

Several hours later and Sawyer and Lexi stood on the steps of the farmhouse while they watched their guests drive off. Jessica and Baxter were putting Hunter in his car seat so that he could spend the night with them. Both Lexi and Sawyer walked to the car to say goodbye to their son. He had no issues going with his grandparents and it had been a regular thing since he'd been born.

"You're not in the office this week right?" Baxter said to Lexi.

"Of course not," she sighed, "But if you need me..."

"Lexi, I don't want to hear a thing about work for a week! The firm will still be standing when you return, Mrs McGuire!" he said firmly before he pulled her into a hug. "I love you Peanut," he sniffed before releasing her.

"For the love of God Baxter, she's married, not leaving forever," Jessica came up behind him pressed a kiss to Sawyer's cheek and hugged her daughter then dragged her husband into the car. They stood and watched them drive off.

Sawyer turned to his wife and quickly bent to toss her over his shoulder. She yelped in surprised and then laughed.

"Husband! Put me down right now!" she yelled in between laughter.

"Not a chance! I've been waiting to

do this all day!" he said.

He opened the bedroom door and then kicked it shut before laying his beautiful wife on the bed. He quickly started removing his clothing in a crazed and animalistic way.

"It was wrong for you to request we not see each other the night before, woman!" he growled as he climbed over her.

"It seems I'm a bit overdressed, husband," she smiled.

Sawyer growled, "Whatever am I going to do with you?"

"I can think of a couple of things," she said slyly.

Sawyer yanked her up and unbuttoned her white lace dress and watched it fall to her feet. She stood before him in a white thong with little bows on the hips and silver stilettos. She moved to slip out of the shoes and Sawyer stopped her.

"Leave them," he ordered as he grabbed her hips and brought her to the bed. She crawled on top of him and placed slow sensual kisses up his chest before their lips crashed together and Sawyer gripped her ass.

"I wanted to talk to you about something," Lexi whispered as she peppered kisses on his neck.

"Now you wanna talk? Damn it, woman, you know I'd give you whatever you asked right now," he huffed as his hand roamed up her curves.

"I want to have another baby," she rushed out.

"I'm working on it," he countered, "but yes, I want another baby too. So how about you stop teasing and let me love you, Mrs McGuire."

A Sneak Peek of *"The Wounded Heart of a Cowboy"*

RELEASING SEPTEMBER 1, 2020

Chapter 1

DANI

8 MONTHS AGO

No one ever expected a female to become a Navy Seal. They said females were incapable of meeting the physical requirements to pass the BUD/s. Many women had tried but none had succeeded. Until her... Dani was determined to put her hands on the Trident Pin and it was that drive that made her damn good at her job.

The guys who trained with her didn't hold back any punches when it came to training. She had to be a superb soldier with outstanding marksmanship and stamina to fall into step with them. It hadn't been an easy task, but the day she was assigned to her team, she knew she'd found a home.

She couldn't have asked for a better group to work with and she always knew they'd cover her six no matter what. They were family and the guys weren't bothered by the fact that she was a woman. They often sought her advice on their relationships or lack thereof. They adopted her as a sister and she loved them as brothers.

She served in the Navy for five years before she decided to give the BUD/s a try. It was an accomplishment. Not just for her, but for other women who saw being a SEAL as an unattainable goal. She'd set the precedent and hoped that more women would start to see the SEALs differently.

At twenty-six years old, Dani had served in Afghanistan and had done high profile jobs in a variety of different locations. The team consisted of six SEALs and one Lieutenant Commander who oversaw their squad. Their fearless leader, Sam Kincaid, was a world-class asshole at times but secretly a softie. He was married until he joined the SEALs ten years ago and had two young daughters at home. Being in the NAVY took a toll on his marriage and other relationships. We pledged a commitment to our country and it took priority in our lives.

The other five SEALs on the team were, Boner (not his real name, but everyone already called him that. Don't ask.), Teddy, Luke, Ethan and Dex. All of them extremely attractive, but Dani couldn't look at them romantically. They were her brothers, if not in blood then in heart.

"You ready, kid?" Dex asked as he clasped her shoulder before they jumped out a cargo plane into an unknown location in the middle east.

Dex was twenty-five years old with a spunky attitude, tattoos covering a large part of his body and he liked to play up his bad-boy persona when he wasn't working. Standing at six-four and built like a UFC fighter with his brown hair and big doe eyes, he had no trouble getting the attention of any woman he wanted.

"Yeah, I'm good! You ready, partner?" Dani said into her helmet, which held their communication device.

Dex winked before giving her a

thumbs up. With that, he jumped out the rear in Dex style. A couple flips thrown in for good measure. Dani hated jumping out of planes, but sometimes it was a necessary evil.

"He's such a dumbass," Sam muttered as he came to stand by her at the end of the rear opening.

"Yeah, but he's ours and we can't return him," she chuckled.

"Trust me, Kid, I've tried," Sam smirked and motioned for the remainder of the crew to prepare to jump. It was him, Dani and Ethan pulling up the rear.

The jump was uneventful and Dani always felt a bit nauseous until she was certain her parachute would open without issue. She thought how stupid it would be if she died while jumping out of the sky after all the work she'd done to get where she was in her life.

She landed before Sam and Ethan and released her chute. The night vision goggles allowed her to see better in the night and she immediately went on guard as soon as her feet touched the sand.

"Harper we're about ten clicks from you to your north," Dex was heard through her comms.

"En route," Dani replied as Sam and Ethan banded together. They were in enemy territory and were tasked with interrupting a terrorist plot. Intel had advised that there was a small group of a local terrorist branch called the Muharib who had been planning to bomb the US embassy in Sudan.

The crew came together and went through the plans for their attack. They weren't certain on how many Muharib were in the confined building or the level of explosives they could have in their possession. A chopper was set to retrieve the team once the task was complete.

They spilt into their assigned teams, each with their task. Dani's team, which included Dex, Ethan and Sam would raid the compound. Ethan had experience with explosives and Dex was a damn fine marksman. They had used the fact that she was a woman to their advantage at times, especially when they used women and children for suicide bombers was becoming more prevalent. The enemy underestimated a woman's value as a possible threat and she had been able to infiltrate many groups and gather intel that a man would never have been able to do.

Comms went silent as they approached the warehouse, which was a shack in the middle of the desert. It comprised of three stories with a large barrier surrounding it for protection. There was a watchman assigned on top of the barrier and Dex was assigned to take him out once Sam, Ethan and she had approached.

They glided as a unit along the wall and Sam gave Dex the signal. They knew once the guard was down that alarms would be tripped. They only had seconds to infiltrate and eliminate the threat.

From above the sound of a body hitting wood was heard. Dex had done his task and now it was their time. Shouts were heard in Arabic as they breached the door. Ethan had placed two explosive devices on either side to cause a small controlled explosion would break through.

We gained entry and were immediately caught in the line of fire. There had to be at least a dozen Muharib. Sam took out the first room as she and Dex cleared the remaining first floor. She took no excitement from ending another human's life, but in these circumstances, the act was justified. She and Dex took out another three on the first floor before collecting Sam and Ethan to storm the second. Once they reached the top of the stairs, they flanked into groups of two. One person always covering the six while the other led. Dex covered her as she cleared two more rooms and took out three more hostiles.

They were able to clear the three floors but had not found anything to suggest a terrorist plot of any kind.

"What the fuck?" Sam bellowed into his comms.

"We're missing something," Dani replied. There had to be more to the assignment. Surely, they wouldn't have been sent if they didn't have the correct information.

"Luke," Dani said, "is there a basement?"

"If there is it wasn't on the blueprints or previous recon," Luke said from his perch outside the compound. They were covering from a distance with sniper rifles.

"What is it, Dani?" Sam questioned.

Dani had completed several missions and this one was making her skin crawl. They were missing something.

"When we made entry, I noticed there was a small tarp covering an area outside," Dani said.

"Fuck," Sam cursed.

The team made their way out of the house and approached the tarp Dani spotted. Sam gave her the go-ahead to lift the tarp and she found a small door that led under the house. It wasn't a large hole and she was certain that the men behind her would not be able to fit through.

"I'm going in," Dani exclaimed.

"Now Kid, let's talk about this. You go in there and you're it. We can't get in there if something goes wrong. We can't cover your six in there and I don't like it," all traces of the fun-loving man Dex was normally was gone, as he stared her down.

"And if we don't get in there and get the information, we lose it all and risk a terrorist plot proceeding. I'm going in Dex," she replied firmly.

Dani tossed her rifle over her back and made to assess the hole. It was big enough for her tiny frame and the mere size of the hole would prevent the military from being able to enter.

She turned and nodded to Sam, who gave her the go-ahead.

"Sam, c'mon man, this isn't a good idea," Dex argued as he got in Sam's face.

"Are you questioning my decision making, Petty Officer?" Sam gritted, not backing down from Dex's challenge.

"Boys, boys…" Dani exclaimed, "Dex if this was you, would you take the risk?"

"Dani this isn't me, it's you," he turned to lock eyes with her. She and Dex had become close over the past year working together. He trusted her and she trusted him.

"But you would. Now I have the chance and I'm doing it. There is no argument to be had. Ethan," she pointed to him as he stood to the side. The man knew how to keep quiet and in reality, he was a bit too interested in things that went boom, "stay on comms in case I need your direction with anything I come across?"

"I got your back Harper," Ethan said nodding his agreement.

With that, Dani slid to her belly and using her arms crawled slowly into the small hole. Once past the entrance, Dani was able to see that a room had been dug out and that it was deep enough to allow her to stand.

"Guys..." she called.

"Harper," Sam answered.

"We've got a problem," she admitted as she peered into the small scared eyes of a young girl. Her golden skin was lit by a small flashlight that she held in her hand. In the other, she held a detonator button which was linked to a vest of C4 around her chest.

Dani took in the remainder of the room and the child who stood before her. She was no more than ten years old with a slight frame. Her head was covered and her dress ran to her ankles. Silent tears of fear flowed freely down her cheeks.

"I've got a child in here strapped to a vest of C4," Dani whispered. She was certain she heard Dex swear.

"Dani, I need you to come out here if you can," Sam directed.

"She hasn't pushed the button yet Sam. I can try to talk to her. She's just a child for God's Sake!" Dani said forcefully. She did not take her gun and aim it was the girl. She felt the fear radiating from her as her thumb twitched around the button.

"Dani, get the fuck back here. That's an order," Sam bellowed.

"I'm not here to hurt you," Dani said in Arabic. She'd learnt the language in preparation for training. And boy, did it come in handy.

"Sweetheart, let me help you okay? You don't want to hurt anyone do you?" Dani prompted.

"NOW HARPER!" Sam screamed into comms.

Dani made to approach the girl with her hands up, but it must have been what she was waiting for. Dani saw the change of her expression as she muttered something under her breath in Arabic. Dani quickly shifted and attempted to flee.

She got half her body out of the opening before she heard the child screaming in Arabic.

"GO! GO!" Dani yelled at her team as she slid out of the structure. As soon as she made it out the explosion rang out in the night. Dani's body propelled forward into the hard sand. Her ears rang and she felt a burning in her legs. Dazed she looked down and saw that a large piece of shrapnel, a rod to be exact, had stabbed into her thigh. Dani tried to move but screamed out in pain.

No one prepares for this shit, she thought.

Next thing she knew she was being dragged as she slipped in and out of consciousness. Her helmet came off as she was loaded onto the helicopter.

"Dani! Dani! Open those beautiful eyes for me, darling," Boner drawled in his southern accent. He was the trained medic and was the last voice she heard before she passed out.

Dani woke several days later in a hospital in Florida. There were rods and bolts stuck in her leg. Dani was told that she had been medically discharged as the doctors reported permanent damage to her leg. She'd never have full function, but with physical therapy, she could have a relatively normal life.

Her brothers had made it out fine and were there when she opened her eyes. Concern etched all of their faces. Dex told her about her injury and the prognosis. After they left, Dani cried into her pillow. If she wasn't a SEAL anymore, what was she?

And what was she going to do with her life?

Chapter 2

FINN

PRESENT-DAY

Finn sat on a stool in Daisy's classy establishment, The Barn House. He watched as his sister expertly tossed out drinks and offered smiles to those she knew. The place was packed and Finn decided to indulge in a beer with his brother after the long day they'd had.

Remi was in his glee after marrying the love of his life and was expecting his first child in a couple of weeks. He'd be lying if he said he wasn't jealous. His brothers had done well for themselves. Remi and Sawyer were happy and settled in their new lives and had two beautiful women to keep them in line.

"So, how's my beautiful sister-in-law and soon to be niece?" Daisy asked leaning in to place a kiss to his and Remi's cheeks.

"Honestly," Remi began, "she's a blubbering mess and these cravings and hormones are insane," he sighed as he tipped back his long neck.

"Ah yes, the cravings," Daisy chuckled.

"You laugh now sister, but don't be calling me when you get in the family way and need a Big Mac at 3 am," he said pointing his beer at Daisy.

Finn chuckled from beside Remi, "Yes you poor bastard. You got a beautiful woman who tolerates you and let's be honest... she settled for you. And a beautiful child coming into this world," Finn said sarcastically from his seat next to his brother.

"Excuse me, ma'am? Are these assholes bothering you?" Sawyer's voice boomed from behind. Daisy flicked him a beer with a smile as he took the seat on the other side of Finn.

"Naw, these assholes are fine. It's the

other assholes I worry about," Daisy admitted and Finn heard the exasperation in her voice.

"What other assholes?" Sawyer asked.

Daisy took a deep breath before leaning across the bar towards her brothers.

"I can't seem to keep bartenders. The guys around here get a bit grabby with them and insult the ladies delicate sensibilities," she put her head in her hands and continued. "Just today, Tina quit because Ricky shot her a wink and made a pass at her," she huffed.

"Not all ladies were brought up like you Daisy. You can take care of yourself, but you'd be hard-pressed to find any fancy pants debutant tolerating that," Remi argued.

"I think you need to find yourself a male bartender," Finn offered.

"I have male bartenders, but I need them to be around in case things get out of hand. They can't be everywhere, and I can't find all-male staff," Daisy argued.

"You need a hand until you hire

someone?" Sawyer asked.

"No, I still have enough to get around. But I need to find someone, so if you know anyone looking, send them my way," she asked.

"Will do little sis. I'll be sure to send all the debutants this way," Sawyer joked and Daisy flipped him off before making her way down the other end of the bar.

A strong hand clapped Finn on the back, "Well if it isn't McGuire," a burly voice boomed through the bar. He'd know that voice anywhere and it instantly put a smile on his face.

"Ethan Ross," Finn said turning to face his friend. Finn and Ethan had gone through high school together. After graduation, Finn enlisted in the Army, but Ethan went on to the Navy where he specialized in explosives and eventually made his way into the elite Navy SEALs. Finn heard he'd returned and was working with Sawyer at the Sheriff's department but hadn't had the opportunity to chat.

Finn rose and gripped the man in a brotherly hug followed by Remi moving aside for Ethan to take his spot.

"It's cool, man. I've just been summoned to pick up a quart of ice cream. Apparently, my soon to be daughter already requires Ben and Jerry's," Remi sighed before waving to his brothers.

Ethan chucked from beside Finn, "He's already wrapped around Charlie's little finger and the sweetheart ain't even born yet."

"Ain't just Charlie, that man would do anything for Aubrey," Daisy said as she moved up to Ethan and handed him a beer. She shot him a wink before she placed a kiss to his cheek, "Welcome home E," she said to him. Finn didn't miss the blush that crawled up his friend's cheeks as he watched Daisy move away to deal with some patrons.

"What brings you down here tonight, Ross?" Finn asked.

"I'm meeting a fellow SEAL, Dani. I figured this was as good a place as any," Ethan said.

"One of your brothers?" Finn asked.

Ethan smirked before he tipped the

beer to his lips, "Yeah, one of the best. Dani is badass and my ass would have been dead a couple of times had it not been for Dani covering my six."

Finn knew the strength of the brotherhood soldiers had with one another. He'd felt that throughout his time in the Army. They relied on each other more than others and when you lost one of your brothers, you felt it in your soul. A man never really came back from war. Not fully.

With that Ethan's phone rang and he motioned that he would step out back to take the call. Finn's eyes were quickly drawn to a newcomer to the bar. She stepped in through the door and all his attention was fixated on her. He'd had his fair share of female company and relationships over time, but there was something about her that just drew him in.

Her long chestnut hair was pulled back in a braid that reached the middle of her back. She wore military boots, black faded skinny jeans which accentuated her long curvy legs. She had curves for days and the swell of her breasts was barely hidden in a skin-tight black tank and a black leather jacket.

His eyes soaked her in as he continued to assess the goddess. Her cool complexion was bronzed to perfection. She had beautiful pouty lips that he had the urge to nip and deep blue eyes the colour of the ocean. Their gazes connected and her lip twitched briefly before her facial expression stoned.